DESERT ENCHANTMENTS

STORIES OF THE DJINN DICTATOR

LAURA ENGELHARDT

Join the Fifth Mage War reader list at https://lauraengelhardt.com/ to receive a FREE short story.

ISBN 978-1-957778-05-1 (eBook) | 978-1-957778-06-8 (paperback)

Library of Congress Control Number: 2023921149

Published in Green Village, NJ USA.

Wandering Wave Press

INTRODUCTION

Welcome to the Fifth Mage War series! Whether or not you've read other books in my series, this duology is a perfect entry point into my exciting world of faeries, mages, and weres.

New readers: I may have plunked you down in the middle of the Sahara Desert, but I'm not leaving you out to dry. I wrote these stories so that you could become familiar with the characters, magic system, and politics of my intricate Fifth Mage War world.

Existing fans: I hope you enjoy this deep dive into Arabia before I release the *Arabian Spells* trilogy next year. In my earlier books, characters referred to the "Djinn Dictator" with a mixture of fear and awe. So I'm pleased to offer you this chance to meet the real Khalid.

Recasting Fate takes place in 1907, as the mage Khalid and his sisters battle the latest European invasion. *Djinn Swarm* is set in the present day, after the American delegation arrives in Riyadh. Both stories focus on Amir Khalid, but cover two very different points in his long life.

For this series, I used our planet's existing geography to make it easier for readers to visualize where the characters are in the world without resorting to itsy-bitsy maps.

Despite sharing a similar geography, the people and cultures of the Fifth Mage War Earth are quite different from those of our real world. This is an alternate history, where the existence of faeries and magick has caused the course of human events to diverge substantially from the world as we know it.

Enjoy!

RECASTING FATE

1

THE SAHARA DESERT. 1907

THE RASP of sand dunes shifting beneath the ever-present wind roared in Khalid's ears. He ignored it as he evaluated the dark landscape. A moonless night was a terrible time to cast complex spells, but the desert held immense power. Illuminated by starlight, the ambient magick blanketing the sand glimmered like translucent purple silk atop black wool.

It would have to be enough. At dawn, the magick released by daylight would make the sand shimmer like molten gold. But by casting the spell in the dark, far from the enemy camp, Khalid wouldn't be able to see his djinni dealing out death.

Before the battle at Sabha, he loved watching his enemy fall.

Everything was different now. But this plan was depressingly similar to all their previous plans to win the war. At least this time if the spell modifications failed, he could recast it without taking his own army down with him.

I don't want to die. Khalid straightened, grateful for the wind that stung his eyes and tugged at his protective scarf.

Worrying was a waste of mental energy. The revised djinn spell would work, and his Saaqib tribe would once again prove its worthiness to rule. They needed to end the war quickly — before the other Arabian tribes withdrew their fighters. A bloodless victory tonight would offset the price of winning Sabha.

Or so his sisters believed.

The wind gusted past, bringing with it painful memories: the sharp copper scent, the dusky red collage painted into the golden sand. The sticky feel of his blood-soaked robes drying in the midmorning heat. The frantic prayers of the small cadre huddled behind him. The screams.

Khalid wrapped his headcloth tighter around his face. *I will kill them all.* And when the European enclaves invaded again, as they always did, he would kill them all again. And again and again. Until the rotten ripeness of the battlefield no longer affected him because it was all he knew.

"Al-Amir, drink this," Malik said.

Khalid turned. He hadn't been expecting Vizier Malik, let alone the four guards the Prime Minister had brought.

"You should be waiting at camp. Out of range," Khalid said, but took the outstretched flagon. A few shots of ambrosia would help him remain conscious after the spell was complete. In truth, he would prefer to pass out and awaken after his djinni had completed their mission. But that was a child's wish, and he was the Amir.

He'd never felt this kind of wracking guilt. A true leader did not murder his own, even unintentionally. And yet, Malik still called him "Al-Amir." His advisor forgave atrocity too easily.

Khalid drank. The fermented silica-salt burned like the desert sun atop already-reddened skin, and he coughed.

"Take your time, Amir," Malik said. "We have hours before sunrise."

"This spell will take at least an hour to cast," Khalid replied, but he sipped more slowly, letting the brew coat his tongue with the honeyed flavor of flowers mixed with mint and spice.

The djinn spell required power, precision, and most importantly, endurance. Feeling the rush of magick percolate through his blood as he drank, he realized how spent he'd been — too worn down physically to cast such a complex enchantment without the aid of sunlight or ambrosia. *Malik saved me again*, Khalid thought.

He held out the flagon to his friend.

"You need it more than I," Malik demurred. But when Khalid jiggled the outstretched bottle, his vizier took it. Malik pulled his face covering off and drank deeply. "From the fields around Riyadh?"

Khalid shrugged. "You're the connoisseur. But it's high-proof. What I needed."

"You shouldn't be here with just a body man," Malik scolded, handing the bottle back. "I brought your guards with me."

"The djinn spell modifications are untested—"

"They'll work," Malik cut him off. "This is a better design than the one you attempted at Sabha. At least I'm here now. You may be the only mage capable of raising a djinn, but even you need ambrosia to keep casting the spells day after day!"

Khalid couldn't deny that. Malik had wanted to stay with him, but Khalid had insisted his vizier go to the northern front instead. His sisters had needed all the mages they could muster, and Khalid's djinni were invincible. That was one argument Malik had to be glad he'd lost. If his friend had come with him to Sabha, he'd be dead alongside everyone else.

Khalid drank deeply, then recorked the bottle. "Any more, and I'll explode."

"Do you remember the time Loujain got too drunk to contain her magick? She almost destroyed the shields over the casting field."

He could hear the smile in Malik's voice. He'd rather be dealing with his little sister's excesses right now.

"I wish we were back in Riyadh. I miss my workshop. Before this started, I was close to creating a seeking djinn spell that wouldn't harm the target."

"Soon, Al-Amir, the invaders will be gone, and we'll be home again."

Khalid nodded. That was the hope.

"Do you want to review the schematic? I can hold it while you cast." Malik beckoned Khalid's body man forward, taking the leather-bound spellbook from him.

"Thanks," Khalid replied. His mundane assistant was skilled, but he couldn't see magick, and Khalid would have to prompt him to turn the page. Malik's help would make it easier to concentrate on the spell.

Even if his enemy figured out what Khalid was casting, they wouldn't be able to defend themselves this time. Tonight, Khalid's djinni would attack anyone tethered by a magical binding.

And every European mage was magically bound to their enclave.

This new djinn design came from old research he'd abandoned decades before this war, back when they were still fighting the Magi. Khalid had originally developed the djinn enchantment as a seek-and-destroy spell: find a specific person and spin them apart. That had been a winning strategy when the Saaqib's enemies had been specific mages, but a less effective one when their enemies were hordes of foreign conquerors. So Khalid had changed the design to shield all who had pledged themselves to the Saaqib tribe from his djinni.

Until Sabha.

Malik opened Khalid's spellbook and cast a low-level illumination spell on it. "We're ready, Al-Amir. This spell targets magical bindings, and none of our people should be affected. The questers are out-of-range, and all our apprentices should be unbound by now."

The multicolored schematic glowed brightly, beckoning Khalid. He was giddy from the ambrosia, but that would wear off quickly. He glanced over the first steps of the spell, which he knew by heart. This wasn't simply a via- or silica-salt enchantment, but a mixture of both forms of spellcraft.

The djinni would emerge from the very air itself, their forms mimicking that of their enchanter. Instructions for their short existence were coded in dense, layered patterns of magick that required more endurance than power to cast. His djinn spell was the only long-range magical weapon in existence, unstoppable and devastating. No one could outrun the wind.

Khalid cracked his neck from side to side and rolled his shoulders back. It all began with a simple left-forward three-turn. The rest of the patterns would rest atop that foundation. It was difficult to keep so many complex patterns distinct and separate before releasing them, but Khalid had been casting variations on this spell since 1728. Even exhausted, he could focus long enough to raise a single djinn.

He'd learned that at Sabha.

Khalid flipped the pages forward, studying the modified patterns that targeted magical bindings.

If it worked, the djinni would rip the enclave-bound mages apart. The invaders would flee or surrender. Despite their superior weapons, the French mundanes knew they couldn't win the war without mage support.

The Arabian masters had been given six hours to unbind their apprentices. If one or two were missed, that was an acceptable price for total victory. Or so he tried to convince himself.

This was nothing like Sabha.

Khalid turned the pages back to the beginning of the spell schematic. Malik didn't rush him, didn't say anything to break his concentration. The mundane guards scanned the distance for threats, unaware of the danger Khalid himself posed to them if his first casting failed.

But Malik knew. The vizier's face glowed dimly in the reflected illumination from the spellbook. If this modification didn't work, and Khalid had to cast another djinn — an *unrestricted* djinn — then the price of five mundanes and two mages was an acceptable trade-off.

In theory.

"Your design is sound," Malik said, the cool confidence in his tone audible despite the gusting wind.

Khalid pushed his doubts aside and pulled on his power. Swirls of gold and silver flickered in a forward conical pattern as he built the djinni. He allowed himself the pleasure of getting lost in its glorious complexity. This was the scaffolding on which the functional aspects of the enchantment would rest. It was difficult magick, requiring multiple layers of patterns and tempos to bend the desert air.

Malik flipped the page.

Khalid adjusted the timing of the rippling pattern in the lower quadrant before moving on to the next stage. Methodically, slowly, he built the djinni, encoding the task his creations would undertake in each line of the undulating magick.

He smoothed the edges of the final pattern in the design. At this point in a multi-djinn casting, Khalid normally struggled to maintain visual focus, but right now, he could see the dense lines of his spell without squinting. Either Malik had sourced some extraordinarily high-proof ambrosia, or Khalid had made a mistake. Khalid hesitated, staring at the intricate turns of magick.

"I see no errors, Amir," Malik announced.

How well he knows me, Khalid thought, and held his breath as he released the spell.

The first djinn emerged in the night sky: a whirlwind topped with a simulacrum of Khalid himself. Knife-sharp grains of sand spun upward, pulled by the centrifugal force of the air that formed the construct's lower half. Khalid swallowed down bile as he looked at his creation. The djinn's outstretched arms were frozen in a gesture of welcome, but its unblinking eyes were indifferent to the suffering it was about to cause.

If only he could create a living construct, he wouldn't be forced to watch oversized statues of himself wreaking destruction. Before Sabha, he used to revel in the fact that his enemy would know *he* had been the mage who had killed them. Now, the sight of his giant face in the sky made him sick.

Two more djinni coalesced, dragging roiling storms of colored lightning behind them like fringed capes. Malik shut the spellbook, words of congratulations on his lips. But his face fell, his compliments silenced before they could be uttered. Khalid's heart rate sped up as he followed his vizier's gaze.

The three djinni should have been flying north over the dunes to the enemy encampment, spinning tornados of wind and lightning beneath them. Instead, the constructs hung suspended in midair, their lower whirlwinds frozen into a stillness as eerie as their unmoving humanoid tops.

A rush of air rippled Khalid's headscarf and robe, but the desert was suddenly silent. He could no longer hear the rasp of wind over sand.

Eurus, Khalid realized, his grim fear sinking into actual dread.

The glimmering white-gold outline of a woman's face emerged in front of the djinni. Khalid swallowed as she pressed her lips against one statue-like face before dissipating back into air.

Khalid waved Malik back to the assembled guard. "Go," he said. "Back to camp."

But Malik pressed shoulder-to-shoulder with him. "No one can contend against the air itself, Amir. It won't matter if we stay or go."

That's an unfortunate truth, Khalid thought. For all they knew, Eurus existed within the very air they drew into their lungs. She was everywhere but only rarely took physical form. Humans, even other faeries, were typically beneath her notice.

"Your djinni still don't live."

The East Wind's soft voice was impossible to locate, though they all spun around to look for her. Eurus *was* air, an elemental faerie born billions of years ago when the Earth's atmosphere formed.

"Why are you here?" Khalid called, his voice overly loud in the stillness.

Eurus, as the East Wind liked to be called, manifested into a shadowed figure floating cross-legged as if atop a flying carpet. But of course, Eurus didn't need any support to defeat gravity.

Khalid's face covering blew off, and he caught the red

headcloth before responding. "You told me war didn't interest you anymore."

"Your djinni interest me." The elemental faerie's voice hovered in the air around him, pressing against him like the atmospheric warning of an approaching sandstorm.

"I'm no via-enchanter to cast spells on living things, Lady Eurus," Khalid reminded her. The fae demanded honesty, and he'd told her this many times already. "I don't know how to make a djinn draw breath."

"You were working hard to modify your spells," Eurus said. "At least until your sisters convinced you to claim the Sahara for your al-Saaqib tribe."

"I have a duty to protect the desert's people. I can't play with spell designs while we remain under threat," Khalid said — then cursed himself when he realized he'd given her an opening.

She pounced. "I am more dangerous than five thousand battlemages. Bargain with me. I can steal your enemies' breath. Blow their ships back from your shores. I can keep your lands safe from the predators while you perfect your djinn spells."

"I'm no via-enchanter, Lady Eurus," Khalid repeated. "I spent decades and only managed to integrate biomarkers into the design."

His gaze flickered up. Six vacant eyes that matched his own stared down at him in impotent stillness. Eurus's magick held his unreleased djinni captive. He needed her to let them fly. Let Khalid kill his enemy.

"You see how well I can keep you safe," Eurus said, glancing upward as well. "Even from your own spells."

Khalid hated how tempting her offer was now. Everyone else had perished at Sabha. It had been a Pyrrhic victory, but a victory nonetheless. If she didn't release his djinni, this battle would end in an actual defeat.

There was nothing worse than defeat.

"Do not surrender, Al-Amir," Malik whispered. "With or without the djinni, we will prevail!"

"Surrender? Who said anything about surrender? I'll be your hired hand, Amir Khalid ibn Hawwa al-Saaqib!" Eurus's voice hung slyly in the air as she fluttered down into a full bow, her thin frame splayed across the sand before him.

Khalid stared down at the elemental faerie. No sane human made a bargain with a faerie, but then, no sane faerie stalked a human.

Eurus was practically a myth. Most of the ancient fae had long since faded back into the elements from which they came. After a dozen disconcerting encounters with the East Wind, Khalid wondered if the only reason she hadn't faded was her hope of one day playing with miraculously self-aware djinni.

But faeries played in forests, not deserts. In fact, Eurus was the only faerie Khalid had ever met. He'd just enchanted his first djinn and was rapidly losing consciousness when Eurus emerged from the air beside it. She'd tried to dance with his construct, her white, pupilless eyes gleaming in the sunlight. But its unmoving arms had disappointed her, and she demanded he make it "live" in that now-familiar, omnipresent voice of hers.

He'd collapsed. When he woke, he assumed she'd been but a dream: the fae didn't venture into the barren deserts. Eurus returned only after the Saaqibs had freed the Arabian desert from the Magi. That time, there was no mistaking her for a dream: she'd remained inchoate, pulling him from his newly-built casting field in Riyadh into the sky. At first, he'd been too surprised to be scared.

She'd coalesced from the air beside him, popping into being with as little effort as it took him to flex his fingers.

"Life is struggle," the East Wind announced, and told him to call her Eurus. "I have only my siblings left to challenge. Set your djinni free to play with me." Then she made her first offer.

Back then, Khalid didn't understand the meaning of a fae bargain. But he'd been too honorable to make a promise he couldn't keep. At the same time, he'd been too proud to admit that creating life was beyond his ability. "Go back to Siberia and play with your own kind," he'd suggested.

"Not even the most powerful seelie queens can contend with the air itself," she replied.

That was the moment Khalid realized how dangerous Eurus was. He tried to appease her, hoping she'd eventually find another pastime or interest. But every few years, she returned. Needling him, extolling his latest developments. *And*, Khalid swallowed, *making offers*.

He removed his outer robe, shaking the sand from it before reaching down to help her up. "Lady Eurus, I'm no via-enchanter to breathe life into my spells. I have no talent for such magicks."

But she knew that already. Eurus had already assured him she was willing to wait. That he would need centuries of study before he could even attempt to bring his mage-construct to awareness. But still she returned, asking for what he knew he couldn't give her — even if he lived longer than Methuselah.

Khalid squeezed her hand and let go, praying she would let him go as well. He held out his robe to her. "Lady, I'm not powerful enough to make the djinni live. I can only disappoint you."

"You delight me," Eurus replied, her pupilless white eyes glistening as she pulled his robe around her. "So honest even when I frighten you with my power! Few faeries can manage that. Even fewer humans."

Still, she didn't leave. Khalid could see no other option. "Let my spell fly, and we can bargain. You aid my enemy by giving them time to understand the enchantment."

"Your djinn spell spins too fast for them to discern," Eurus said in that disembodied voice in his ear. "And even if you gave their elders a perfectly drawn schematic, I doubt they could cast the counterspell."

He knew the East Wind was telling him something important — her voice was heavy with anticipated glee — but Khalid struggled to glean her meaning.

"Why do you hold Al-Amir's djinni back, Lady Eurus?" Malik broke in, giving Khalid time to think. "I thought you loved watching them soar."

"I do!" Eurus flipped backward, an impossible twisting of her body had she been human.

"Then why hold our djinni hostage?" Malik asked.

There was a reason his friend was the Saaqib's prime minister. The wind quieted, and Khalid's pounding heart sounded loud in the sudden stillness.

"I haven't provided you with proof of power before now," Eurus said, gesturing upward to the suspended djinni. "You control your lands only at my whim."

"That's true of everyone, Lady," Malik replied. "No one can live without breath."

"If my spell spins too fast for the European mages to discern, how did they figure out how to escape my djinni at Sabha?" Khalid asked, beginning to understand her game.

A fleeting smile of satisfaction ran across Eurus's face. She was playing with him.

"I told them." She swayed joyfully from side to side as if buffeted by countervailing winds. "They couldn't believe protecting themselves from the djinni could be as simple as declaring themselves members of your Saaqib tribe! But I'm fae and cannot lie, so they did it. Of course, they betrayed their own familial oaths and so got what they deserved."

Eurus couldn't lie, but her truths were twisted with misdirection.

"*My* army didn't deserve death," Khalid said, trying to keep the accusation from his voice. Despite his aversion to the elemental faerie, he'd thought they had an understanding. That she held him in some esteem.

"Elder André offered me quite a bit to learn the secret to avoiding your spell. Bargained away his enclave's *future* for that one little detail."

Eurus sounded pleased by that. Though with everyone at Sabha dead, Khalid wasn't sure how she'd be able to collect.

At Sabha, Khalid had been shocked when his djinni spun aimlessly through the enemy camp, leaving the enemy legions untouched. Their magick faded without them destroying anything. He didn't dare waste more time wondering how the European mages had discovered the secret of safeguarding their soldiers. Instead, he'd made a "battlefield judgment," as his sisters called it.

Gambling was what he called it. He'd gambled with his people's lives, and lost. Khalid had known he wasn't strong enough to take down a dozen enclave battlemages alone so he'd conjured a single djinn to destroy all in its range. He should have known he wouldn't be fast enough to counter an unrestricted djinn in time.

But he'd gambled on his ability to finish casting the counterspell before his one djinn could finish dismembering the enemy army. He'd set that whirlwind loose, only to be shocked into stillness by the sight of his own unblinking eyes as the djinn ripped through his own people.

That one djinn had been much faster, much stronger

than he'd realized. By the time Khalid managed to decompose the spell, he was the sole survivor.

"You're always so cautious when we speak," Eurus said. "You surprised me when you didn't order a retreat after your djinni dissolved into wind."

"I had little time to decide," Khalid retorted, his heartbeat speeding up. *I should have ordered a retreat.* He didn't need her reminding him about things he wished he could forget.

As he'd twisted the final red-gold lines of the disenchantment, the djinn had been so close, he'd felt its electric gusts. *All gone.* Khalid swallowed down the remembered copper tang. He needed a bloodless victory tonight to atone for the thousands he'd lost at Sabha.

"Al-Amir knows we must crush the Europeans completely so that they will finally stop trying to claim our deserts. Ordinary defeat just sends them home to regroup and return. To retreat would have been a mistake." Malik sounded so certain.

Khalid wished he could absorb his vizier's faith. He rolled his shoulders back, forcing the memories away. "I see your power, Lady Eurus. If I bargain with you in good faith, will you let my djinni fly once we have completed our discussion?"

"That would be fair." Eurus pulled her feet beneath her to sit atop the air cross-legged again. "Agreed."

"Agreed," Khalid repeated, trying to stop thinking about what Eurus had done, would do, if she didn't get what she wanted. He started to sit atop the sand when Eurus sent the wind to raise him up.

Both Malik and Khalid settled onto the air. The wind stilled around them as if they were cocooned in a stone-walled palace.

Eurus nodded at him.

Of course. It was his "turn." She had made the first offer: Eurus would keep Arabia safe if he agreed to spend his life developing a spell to make his djinn constructs live. Expend it, really: great magick required great sacrifice. But even if he were willing to sacrifice himself for Arabia's safety, he didn't have the magical power or know-how to cast such a spell.

She opened with a deal she knew I would turn down, Khalid mused, wishing he could consult Malik without Eurus listening. *She expects me to counter.*

"I don't want you bargaining with my enemies," Khalid announced, watching for her reaction. It had to be the request she expected after her opening salvo.

The wind ruffled Eurus's hair, blowing it upward so its pale strands fanned out like a rippling crown. "Wouldn't you rather leave Arabia's defense to me and focus on your spelling? You just told your vizier how much you longed to be home in your workshop."

Khalid hated how she listened to his conversations. Nothing spoken aloud was secret from the very air itself. He hated her almost as much as he hated himself. And if this bargaining dragged out too long, he feared he might tell her just that.

"I'm too weary to play these games, Lady Eurus," Khalid said. "You've proven your willingness to trade with my enemies. You've reminded me of your power. If you side with the invaders, none of my spells can defeat them. I understand the stakes. Just tell me what you want."

"Come to Delphi with me and petition the Oracle for a prophecy."

Khalid blinked. "What? Why?"

Eurus's amused chuckle tickled his ears.

"My brother says you glow with a burgeoning prophecy. Come to Delphi so the Oracle might read it."

"Your brother?" Khalid grasped for something familiar, something he could understand.

"My younger brother, Zephyr. Not Boreas," Eurus's mouth flexed in a pout. "Boreas plays his own games."

The last thing Khalid wanted was more elemental faeries blowing across his deserts.

"Are you bargaining for all the winds, then?" Malik asked.

"Boreas isn't interested in you or your lifeless deserts," Eurus replied. "But Zephyr has lost his zest for living. I invited him to examine your djinni to see if he might be excited by their potential. He finally came to watch you cast at Sabha."

Khalid's gut burned with a fury he couldn't quite contain. It leaked into his voice. "Is that why you bargained with the European enclaves? To make sure I'd cast again? You—"

Malik pressed one shoulder against his, and Khalid stopped speaking.

Eurus shook her head. "I knew you'd cast again. I *thought* you'd sound a retreat, spend a few months tweaking your spell. But you're more of a gambler than I supposed. It was a near thing. I was about to blow you away when you managed to disenchant it."

Khalid swallowed hard. If Eurus had saved his life, she would own it now. "I don't want any part of your family games."

"This is no game," Eurus said sharply. "I don't contend with my siblings. It's one of the reasons why I like you. Why I like your people. You keep faith with your sisters."

"What do you and your brothers stand to gain if we go and petition the Oracle?" Malik asked.

"Not you!" Eurus's eyes flashed iridescent with her rebuke. "Khalid must come alone. If Zephyr can't manage to change the future, then Khalid must be the sole petitioner so that he gains enough power to make his djinni live."

Change the future? Khalid thought. Perhaps this was not as simple as he'd thought. Fae bargains never were.

"How would Al-Amir gain power?" Malik asked.

Malik was falling into her trap. The real question was what Eurus stood to gain by this. She had gone to a great deal of trouble to orchestrate it. *Why,* Khalid wondered.

"Speaking a prophecy releases a pivotal power," Eurus declared. "Does Khalid make a petition, and the Oracle reads his fate, then will he leave Delphi *coated* with magick."

Starlight glinted off the elemental's sharp chin and cheekbones like the edges of a knife. "Dripping with power," she added.

"But saddled with a prophecy." Khalid shook his head. "Only fools visit Delphi."

"Many fools," Eurus agreed. "Those who know their future but cannot change it have no hope. It's why we Winds shed the power of prediction when we emerged from the air molecules inside that cave. But what if fate *can* be changed?"

"You were born at Delphi?" Malik asked.

"An elemental isn't born," the East Wind corrected him. "We first manifested at Delphi."

"That's why the air in those caves is so full of magic," Malik said.

Eurus nodded, floating up and down with glee.

She thinks she has me, Khalid thought. "But I don't need more power," he said aloud. "So this is not a fair bargain."

"But you *need* me to ignore your enemies! Their proposition at Sabha was not the first time they made an offer."

Malik tilted his head, considering her. "But they don't have anything that you want."

The air around them stilled, but the East Wind didn't speak.

"What do you want, Lady Eurus?" Khalid asked.

Her blank eyes glittered in the starlight as she fixed her gaze on the frozen spell hanging overhead. "I want Zephyr to get a restart. A rebirth. He doesn't find your lifeless djinni appealing, and doesn't find anyone else's struggle interesting enough to manifest. So I issued him a challenge: change the future. It's the only thing he's shown any interest in lately."

Khalid heard a tremble in her voice. For the first time, he thought he understood her. Like him, Eurus loved her siblings.

"Why do you need Amir Khalid for this?" Malik asked.

"Because we need a prophecy against which he can contend. After seeing you at Sabha, Zephyr chose yours."

"But prophecies aren't prognostications," Khalid said. "They can't be changed."

Eurus nodded her agreement. "Once they take shape, that's true. Of course, it takes time to spell a prognostication into prophecy, just as it takes time to spin air into a djinn. Zephyr thinks he remembers enough of our magick to unravel the Oracle's spell before it is fully set."

"A worthy challenge," Malik agreed, his eyes flickering to Khalid and back. "If your brother succeeds, Al-Amir's future will remain malleable. Zephyr will have fought fate itself to a standstill."

"And if Zephyr fails," Khalid added slowly, understanding the insidious bargain she proposed. "I will be the unlucky pivot point in an Oracular prophecy."

"With all the power that comes from being a pivot!" Eurus's voice was sharp enough to etch glass.

Khalid wasn't immune to the mage-craving for more power. But being tormented by a future you couldn't change was even worse than being haunted by the past. What good was a future without hope?

"We should meet your brother," Malik said.

Eurus sawed back and forth, her angular body twisting unnaturally in the air. "That is your right. Of course, he's already in Delphi, working on his spells." She smiled. "We ought to drag this bargaining out. Zephyr is finally enjoying himself again. Anticipation is the spice of life."

Khalid spoke without thinking. "No!" He looked at his suspended spell. They were so close to victory. He needed this war to be over. And perhaps if her brother were a better playmate, Eurus might lose interest in his djinni.

He stood up on air that felt more solid than sand. Malik scrambled to stand up beside him.

"I'll go," Khalid said. "I will visit the Oracle, petition for a prophecy. And neither you nor your brothers will ever bargain with my enemies again."

"Neither of my brothers has any interest in your enemies or the deserts you fight over. I can speak for us all. Are we agreed?"

"But only after we drive the invaders out. I won't go before then," Khalid added one last condition.

"Done." Eurus's omnipresent voice echoed in the stillness.

"Done," Khalid responded with far less gusto.

Her sharp face relaxed into an almost tender expression. "Prophecies are not worth the power they promise. But I think Zephyr can succeed. I'll even protect him so he can focus solely on his casting. And if you *are* saddled with a prophecy, I'll help you make the best of it."

A gust of wind blew Malik back a step. "But you must remain here."

As Malik nodded, Eurus's form dissipated in a breeze that ruffled their robes. In a heartbeat, they stood on the shifting sand, the rasp of wind across the dunes signaling the East Wind's departure.

Khalid held his breath as the multicolored mosaic in the sky began to move. The lightning crackled, and the whirlwinds corkscrewed, propelling the three djinni forward in an implacable advance. Bright plumes of color shone in their wake as they spun across the sand toward the enemy camp.

The deal was done. The war, won. And while fae bargains had a way of going wrong, Khalid was too tired to worry about that now.

"Bring me back a bottle of Greek wine," Malik murmured as the pair stared at the swirling djinni.

2

DELPHI, GREECE

THE JUNIOR DEVOTEE kept answering questions Khalid hadn't asked, prattling on about minor elements of the ritual until Khalid wished the East Wind would blow in and steal the man's breath.

"—and the only mages allowed in the caves are petitioners and those chosen to serve as Oracle during a ritual. This is for your protection, of course."

"A sensible precaution," Khalid murmured. The magick contained in Delphi's caves was rumored to exceed that found in Arabia's Empty Quarter.

"I must caution you against using mage sight, Amir Khalid." The junior devotee was now repeating himself like a true pedant. "It's far too dangerous."

Khalid held up his hand. "I recall your warning."

"Our first obligation is the protection of the mages who serve, then the safety of those who petition," the devotee said piously.

"And what of the winds, whose magick created the Fate that you worship?" Khalid couldn't help but needle the officious man.

The devotee shook his head. "The winds are not our concern. They abandoned these caves eons ago. How did you even know that—"

"How much longer until the Oracle is ready?" Khalid glanced toward the door to the monastery's courtyard. He'd been forced to listen to the man for almost an hour.

The devotee's vague answer made it clear that he had no idea, so Khalid professed the need for solitude to prepare for the prophetic rite. The devout chatterbox couldn't argue with that.

Suppressing a sigh of relief, he escaped outside to admire the view of Mount Parnassus from the monastery's courtyard.

The Mediterranean air was still damp with the misty rain that had enveloped their boat this morning. Khalid wiped a finger across his forehead, marveling at the droplets that bedazzled his brow like a watery crown. This climate was marvelous, even if it lacked the rich layers of magick emanating from the desert's sand. The fog hadn't affected the steamship crew's ability to dock, and Khalid seemed to be the only person entranced by the abundance of water.

Khalid had spent his first trip across the sea in a bemused state and still couldn't get over the dampness. Even when the sun shone, the air felt pregnant with moisture. Travel was always mind-opening, he supposed, but nothing about this expedition seemed real.

At least, that's how he felt before arriving at Fate's Temple. The older devotee who had taken his tribute was too business-like in her approach to be part of some sort of wistful dream.

Khalid ran his fingers through his hair, marveling at the drops of water that clung to it. While neither Eurus nor Zephyr had materialized during the crossing, he imagined he could feel their presence in the thick air. Or perhaps that was just this odd humidity.

As if summoned by his thoughts — though thankfully Khalid knew that feat was beyond her ability — Eurus's disembodied voice pressed around him.

"The devotees are overwrought. Their mages see the sparking of a major prophecy about you, so Pythia herself will oversee the ritual."

Khalid wondered if the senior devotee's attendance would make it harder for Zephyr to usurp their prophetic rite, but Eurus didn't sound worried. Of course, the East Wind didn't have much to lose in the game she had gone to such trouble to organize.

"Do you still want me to make the petition?" Khalid whispered. His hand instinctively brushed over his right pocket where he'd placed his speech. He didn't relish explaining the Saaqib's plans to secure Arabia's borders to a foreigner, even a devotee of the Oracle. But doing so was part of the petitioning process.

"Yes. Pythia won't be able to abort the ritual once you and the Oracle enter the caves," Eurus said. "The air down there is too powerful. Now that they've been selected, I'll breeze down and see if the atmosphere below has already started to change." She sounded excited.

Khalid glanced around the courtyard. The mist limited his range of vision, which must be why he felt anxious. A mage could only cast as far as they could see. Of course, he wasn't supposed to cast anything today. Beyond speaking his petition, he wasn't supposed to do anything at all.

Still, he felt uneasy. Devotees bustled back and forth between the temple and the monastery. He couldn't hear them, but he felt their attention, their banked excitement. Khalid turned to look out at the mist-covered mountains.

Their lush greenery was coated in fiery licks of magick

emerging from the gray clouds. This landscape was breath-takingly beautiful in its own way. He didn't miss the glorious multicolored glow of his deserts as much as he'd feared.

The wind gusted, brushing droplets of mist from his hair.

"Are you planning to remain hidden in the air, too?" Khalid asked. He had no real expectation of receiving an answer, so was a little surprised when a baritone voice responded.

"It's easier to cast complex spells in material form. I'll appear after we enter the cave." Zephyr's disembodied voice was a breath of watery wind in the misty air.

"You just don't want to attract the devotees' notice until it's too late," Khalid whispered.

A soft chuckle grazed his ear.

"I wondered why my sister put so much faith in you. Perhaps you think better when you're not under pressure."

Khalid raised an eyebrow. He didn't care what this bored, near-suicidal elemental thought of him. He only hoped that Zephyr's "rebirth" would free him from the East Wind's attention.

"Eurus proposed this challenge to entertain you. Perhaps you might design one for her," Khalid said.

The faint outline of a translucent face, visible only to mage-sight, appeared in the mist. Zephyr wasn't as gaunt as his sister, though his features were just as sharp.

"Should we see which of us can grow the largest sand-storm?" Zephyr asked.

"If you think she would find that entertaining." Khalid refused to be goaded by the elemental's malice. At least his omnidirectional voice was less disconcerting now that Khalid could see him.

A smile glinted on Zephyr's square face. "You are bold, but not as foolish as I thought. Good!"

It was as if Zephyr was testing him, which concerned Khalid.

"Why does it matter whether I'm bold or foolish? All I have to do is make my petition."

"Hijacking the future is impossible. Or so everyone believes," Zephyr replied. "I have the skill to dissolve a prophecy, but perhaps not enough power. And, of course, you're the wild card."

"The wild card?" Khalid asked.

"This is a tricky casting. The Oracle will be too caught up in channeling the cave's magick, but you might well fight to hold onto the power that comes to you." Zephyr's face dissolved into mist. "They're bringing the mages into the caves now."

"At last," Khalid murmured.

"Amir Khalid, all has been prepared."

Khalid turned. Beside the overly chatty devotee stood a tall woman with a pale complexion and sliver-streaked black hair. Her indigo cloak and yellow dress were heavily embroidered with metallic thread that caught the dim sunlight. Droplets of water clung to the patterns like diamonds. Magick had been trapped by the rain, and swirls of glorious color lit each orb with the wealth of the deserts.

Conquest was the lazy mage's choice. If he were a European mage, he would concentrate on developing spells to wring the dissolved silica-salt from the rain, not planning invasions. But he wasn't a European mage. Or a bored faerie.

"I'm Pythia, Fate's senior devotee," the tall woman announced in a tone that made clear Khalid should feel deeply honored. "I will *personally* be officiating the rite of prophecy today."

"I'm ready," he said.

Pythia turned toward the temple, brushing the rain droplets from her shoulders. Khalid's breath caught at the waste.

3

DELPHI, GREECE

FATE'S TEMPLE SAT atop the crevice that led down into the caves. The exterior walls were studded with massive windows set inside gilt frames. Gold and silver inlay gleamed from every available surface. Khalid suspected that the temple would glow like a beacon on a sunny day.

Pythia pushed the ornately carved door open and led him toward the stairwell in the center of the temple. A gilt railing circled the entry to their holy site, but it was otherwise unguarded. There didn't appear to be any leakage of magick from the cavern below; only the barest smattering of color clung to the white marble floor. This land might be rich in water, but it was poor in ambient magick.

Convex mirrors studded the pillars and walls so that the temple's interior was brightly lit. Pythia paused at the railing and pointed at the four fluted columns closest to the stairs. Large, angled mirrors reflected Khalid's face down at him. He looked away. They reminded him too much of his djinni.

"There are mirrors in the caves below just like these," the senior devotee said proudly. "Only the petitioner, the officiant, and the Oracle are permitted underground during the session. But our devotees know how to adjust the mirrors up here to keep the cavern illuminated. We don't need gas lamps, even on a dark day like today."

"Impressive," Khalid said, because that was obviously what she wanted to hear.

She nodded, pulling the gate open and gesturing for him to precede her down the broad gold staircase. The spiral was wide enough across that a skilled pilot could guide a standard two-person carpet through the tight space.

The temperature dropped as Khalid descended, and a cold breeze cut through his outer robe. Pythia was right; the mirrors augmented the light from above, so Khalid could see the unadorned gray limestone of the cavern as clearly as if they weren't two stories underground.

He'd been careful to keep his vision confined to the mundane spectrum while descending, ruthlessly suppressing the urge to use his mage-sight. Delphi's architects had cut the typical rise of the stairs in half, and it would be an inauspicious start to the ritual if Khalid tumbled into the cave. But when he reached the bottom, he couldn't resist using his mage-sight to peek at the elementals' birthplace.

He braced himself against the rumored intensity of the cavern's ambient magick but was nevertheless unprepared for the shock. Khalid staggered as the vibrant wealth of sensation stole the breath from his lungs. The cave was utterly bathed in moving color. Rich umber shades competed with swirls of iridescent pastels. Sparkles of metallic greens danced in an ever-changing pattern around the room until he grew dizzy.

The scent of ripe pomegranates and dates tripped across his tongue, and Khalid's knees buckled.

"You were warned," scolded Pythia as she reached from

behind to steady him. "Mundane sight only! Unless you plan to abandon Arabia and become an acolyte, you must limit yourself while in the caves."

"I couldn't resist," Khalid replied ruefully, oscillating his sight back to mundane vision. He lurched forward to grip a stalagmite for support. His ears were still ringing from his brief exposure to the concentrated magick. It was indeed more intense than the Empty Quarter.

The sight of the cavern's bland and barren gray walls soothed his palate, and Khalid ran a finger across the cool stone. *Like eating sorbet after an overly rich course.* He was glad they hadn't gilded the surfaces down here.

Be bold but not foolish, he reminded himself. Sometimes it was hard to tell the difference.

The winds' birthplace was full of raw magick, neither channeled into silica-salt nor filtered through the elements. It was a wild and pure power. Little wonder that the three humans who comprised the Oracle rarely spoke unless in trance: they were addicted to the sensual overload. Khalid walked forward, pressing his hand flat against the damp wall.

The feel of that magick had been so incredible, he had to stifle the impulse to peek again.

Pythia's robe brushed him as she swept past, pulling a silk rope to draw back the gray curtain that concealed the oversized entry into the inner cavern. "You mages are all alike. No one listens! But your sisters would destroy me if I accepted you into Fate's Order, so don't bother volunteering."

Khalid barked a laugh and pushed off the wall to follow her. "I have a bit more self-control than that."

"That's what they all say," she muttered.

"But Amir Khalid al-Saaqib tells the truth," Zephyr said,

his voice echoing slightly as he manifested in front of Khalid.

Pythia turned around, her eyes widening as she saw the naked elemental. She recovered from her surprise quickly, her face stilling as she reached to unbutton her outer robe.

"Lord Zephyr." Pythia offered the South Wind her robe. "Now I understand the reason for our mages' excitement."

Zephyr smiled, a wide grin splitting his square face. Like Eurus, his eyes lacked irises or pupils, but Pythia didn't seem disconcerted by his alien visage.

"It's been almost a thousand years since my return was prophesized. Your order maintains good records," Zephyr responded, pulling Pythia's robe around his gray shoulders.

Even the most powerful faeries have their limitations, Khalid thought. Neither Eurus nor Zephyr could manage so basic a fae glamour as the illusion of clothing.

"My devotees were united in their belief I needed to personally oversee today's ritual. Given how strongly the magick pulls at him—" Pythia's eyes flickered to Khalid, then back to the thin elemental. "—I thought it might be the start of a prophetic trilogy."

"Great magick doesn't always run in threes," Zephyr said, clapping his hands together. The sound echoed off the stone walls. "I'm going defeat Fate itself today."

Pythia's face twitched, her shoulders tight. "Interfering in our prophetic rite is risky, even for you, Lord Zephyr."

"Taking risks is part of living," Zephyr shrugged.

The faerie seemed indifferent to her veiled threat, which Khalid supposed was better than taking offense. Zephyr could suck the air from Pythia's lungs and watch her suffocate to death on the cavern floor if he felt like it. Khalid wondered if he considered the senior devotee bold or merely foolish.

"What of you, Amir Khalid? Are you willing to take the risk of a prophecy gone awry?" Pythia asked.

"I agreed to come," he said flatly.

Pythia's dark eyes drilled into him. "You'd allow a faerie to waylay the power that should be yours?"

"Influencing a pivot is also risky, Devotee," Zephyr replied before Khalid could answer.

"He's not a pivot yet," Pythia countered.

Khalid didn't like how they argued over him, as if he had some great role to play in this. "I will make my petition. That's all I agreed to do."

"See! He's not as greedy as most mages." Zephyr tilted his head toward Pythia, opening his hands wide. "One lost prophecy won't doom your order, Devotee. I only seek to see if it can be done. Whatever will be, will be as Fate decrees."

"As you wish." Pythia bowed.

Khalid didn't think Zephyr's false piety had persuaded her and wondered how she planned to contend against the wind.

The senior devotee's gaze caught his. "It's easy to disclaim what you don't yet possess. Harder to give it up once you have it." Her dark eyes remained focused on Khalid's face as a wave of cold air swept past.

"We need to begin," Pythia announced, turning sharply enough that her dress spun motes of cave dust behind her. "This way."

The senior devotee walked through the vast opening, and Zephyr followed.

"Don't worry." Eurus's voice tickled his ears, a faint whisper against the whistle of cold air. "At worst, you will leave here saddled with a prophecy, but compensated with the power of a pivot."

"Can a prophecy go awry?" Khalid whispered, but

Eurus didn't answer. He cursed internally. Bargaining with the fae was always a fool's game.

The inner cavern was a large room with three smooth walls forming a triangle around the entry. Floor-to-ceiling mirrored panels in the center of each wall bounced light from the antechamber up to the mirrored ceiling so that the entire room was as brightly lit as the temple above.

Khalid's eyes twitched with the urge to shift into mage sight, but he resisted. Both Pythia and Zephyr seemed to think he had a greater role to play than that of the petitioner. But without his magick, there was nothing he could do. And even if he dared use his magick, he wouldn't know what spell to cast.

Pythia directed Khalid to sit in a wooden chair in the center of the cave, then crossed to stand behind an oversized easel. Both pieces of furniture were bolted to the floor, which was a wise precaution if you were expecting a wind elemental to show up.

Khalid sat. He could see his too-still expression in the mirror across from him, with Zephyr's thin frame hovering over his shoulder. He wished the faerie would move farther away. They weren't working as a team; Khalid was here to make a petition. That was the extent of their bargain.

Pythia tested the clips that fastened the thick paper to the easel, then began methodically testing the points on her pencils. Fate's mundane devotees were skilled artists, trained to sketch while watching the prophesized scenes of the future unfold. While they didn't record the actual words spoken by the Oracle — they considered prophetic speech holy — they did draw the images shown during these rituals.

The senior devotee seemed preoccupied with her artistic preparations, and Khalid wondered if she were also preparing to stop Zephyr. As sharp as her colored pencils were, he doubted they'd be much use in a fight against the wind. But Pythia had recognized the elemental from a prior prophecy. Her order had at least some warning that Zephyr would one day reappear.

Khalid wished he'd had better warning of what was going to happen. He'd had time to research and discuss the ritual with Malik and his sisters, but his preparations seemed inadequate now. This place was beyond anything he had experienced. Even with his sight firmly fixed to the mundane range of vision, he could sense the weight of magick in the air.

Pythia looked at him. "Is the petitioner ready?" she asked in a formal tone.

Khalid was struck with an almost giddy amusement. She was treating this like just another day in Delphi. Ignore the unmanifested wind elemental who was sending random gusts of cold air around the room. Ignore the manifested elemental who planned to upend her order's entire purpose.

But instead of laughing, Khalid merely nodded.

"The petitioner must speak," Pythia admonished.

"I'm ready." Khalid pulled his petition from his pocket. He and his sisters had spent hours with a half-dozen experts crafting the precise speech he would read to elicit the answers none of them thought they needed.

The wind in the room picked up, and Khalid realized that he had broken into a cold sweat.

Pythia opened the ritual, her voice dropping an octave. "Describe your present to the Oracle, and they will describe your future."

She looked expectantly at him, and he obligingly stared down at his script. But his throat was dry. All the moisture in this land, yet his tongue was stuck to the roof of his mouth. He wasn't sure why he felt such terror now. This wasn't a battlefield; the only thing he had to fear was discovering his own fate.

Khalid coughed, clearing his throat, and let the echoes die before beginning to read.

He'd practiced this speech before, knew it was only about nine minutes long. But as he spoke, he felt the passage of eons. The wind ruffled the pages, and Khalid felt like a traitor for sharing his tribe's secrets with these Greek priests. If Zephyr failed, Khalid would need a pivot's power to raise the djinn barrier that would protect Arabia's borders. But if Zephyr succeeded in changing fate, then Khalid would have to destroy Pythia's sketches so that no one would discover their weaknesses.

At last, Khalid finished.

Before he finished tucking his petition back into his pocket, the Oracle appeared from behind the floor-length mirrors. The two women and one man entered silently, their eyes blank as they twisted to the rhythm of the music only they could hear. According to Malik's research, the Oracle would soon begin a wild dance, twisting the cave's prophetic magick into an iron-clad prophecy.

The three were veiled and gloved so that only their faces were visible; their close-fitting red pants and tunics allowed them freedom of movement. Two of them lacked the dewy skin of a high-level mage, but given the abundance of magick that had coagulated in the cave, Khalid supposed it didn't matter how much power they possessed on their own.

They slid languidly about the room as if caressed by the air currents, and while they didn't touch each other, their movements seemed somehow connected. Metallic embroidery glinted on their clothing, and Khalid was tempted to oscillate his sight to confirm that they had indeed chosen the proper shade of red to disguise them from mage-sight.

He shook off the impulse. They were just wearing the traditional garb.

Both Pythia and Zephyr watched the dance without expression, and Khalid suppressed his impatience for the rite to be done. The Oracle might gyrate for minutes or hours — Malik's reports conflicted on the duration of this phase of the ritual — but all agreed that their dance increased in intensity until it was shattered by their speech.

The Oracle danced for several minutes before Khalid realized they were miming spell patterns. He wasn't the first mage to make a petition, so it was strange that the reports didn't mention this.

The three mages clasped their hands together, each lifting a foot over their head, then kicking it down in a modified starfish spiral before spinning away. Khalid's eyebrows raised in disbelief at the odd combinations of spell patterns. An inverted helix, an arabesque bracket, and an inner rocker? No spell he knew used those patterns in their foundation.

Perhaps no one had written about the Oracle's movements aping spell patterns because the patterns made no sense. He frowned as one of the women traced a flocking pattern with her left hand, while the other mimed a paragraph striation that turned the entire sequence into utter gibberish, magically speaking.

If only I dared oscillate my sight, Khalid thought with frustration. He glanced at Pythia. She hadn't picked up her pencil, and her eyes were focused on Zephyr instead of the Oracle. Zephyr, however, was watching the mages closely. His gray face had taken on an avid expression as he turned his head to follow their movements.

The cave wasn't getting warmer, and the sense of damp hadn't changed, but the air was starting to feel heavier. One after the other, the mages continued to dance out patterns that crossed magical disciplines: a bizarre combination of the foundational elements of binding spells, enchantments, and battle-magick.

At last, they shut their eyes in unison, threw their heads back, and bent backward until their red veils grazed the floor.

They paused, and Khalid leaned forward, his mouth parting as he watched. Perhaps it was because he couldn't see the magick they were channeling, but it seemed like they held their awkward poses for longer than humanly possible.

Pythia picked up a pencil and held it poised over the paper.

Three-dimensional images began to appear in the air, as lifelike as any fae illusion. Khalid inhaled sharply. He saw himself and his two sisters. Loujain stood in her casting stance, wearing an odd sand-colored outfit, while Faiza leaned over what might be a table. His own face bore a horrible, stricken expression.

Khalid's heart sank, and he looked in the mirror at Zephyr's reflection. The faerie's pupilless eyes were difficult to read, but his brow was furrowed. Unlike humans, the fae didn't need to see magick to cast. But all spellwork required effort. Zephyr's intent face and stiff posture signified intense concentration.

"*All great magicks run in threes. We are three. Three it must be,*" the Oracle said in unison, their voices blurring with an achromatic tone that came from all directions at once.

This wasn't a standard opening — although many rituals began with a recitation of this or some other clichéd truism. And it wasn't even fully accurate. Great magicks might come in threes, but stabilizing the power required at least a fourth.

Where is my brother's heir? he wondered, looking again at

the Oracle's moving picture. Their mundane brother had died a century before, but they always included his heir in their ruling Quatrone. They were missing their fourth in this image of the future. Faiza's mouth was open in a rictus of a scream, while Loujain pointed at something in the distance, and Khalid's future self covered his eyes.

More pictures bloomed and faded. Khalid saw his desert, but the vehicles traversing it were far more advanced than any the European invaders had brought with them. He saw his djinni blown away in a wash of light, followed by aeroplanes that flew so fast, they sent thunderclaps in their wake. Metal vehicles rolled across the shifting dunes with ease, and the sky bloomed with pink-clouded explosions.

Pythia bit her tongue as she sketched the horror.

Not my desert! Khalid thought futilely. *Not my Arabia!* The carnage he was witnessing was worse than Sabha. It was like a scene out of the Mage Wars fought millennia ago, complete with the kind of devastation that had broken the Gobi and Taklamakan deserts. That now threatened to break his newly-won Sahara. To break the world.

Two enormous djinni emerged from the carnage, bigger than any he had ever constructed previously, but like all the others, they wore his face. Their massive lower whirlwinds spun multicolored lightning around the room, passing through a pink cloud that bloomed like a mushroom, followed by hundreds of miniature clouds of pink, gray, and gold.

The giant djinni spun snow atop a frozen ocean, then flung streaks of colored lighting against broken forests that had been petrified into stone. The hum of life that had somehow been present in the earlier images was gone. No insects, no animals, no faeries, no humans. All that was left was the djinni.

"Victorious!"

All three mages pointed at him. The Oracle's pronouncement raised the hair on the back of Khalid's neck.

"Djinni break deserts free!"

The Oracle's achromatic speech rippled around the room with the same omnidirectional tone of the elementals: this annihilation was his prophecy.

Zephyr's stance remained unchanged, but his fists were white-knuckled with strain. Khalid willed the faerie to succeed; he did not want to be saddled with this future. Even if the Oracle prophesized total victory for Arabia, for him.

Death. Death. Death. All dead.

The ultimate Pyrrhic victory.

Change it, Khalid urged Zephyr silently. *Even if I lose Arabia. Even if I lose everything.*

It was unbearable to be a mere witness. The wind buffeted his shoulders, pressing him back into the chair. Khalid remembered the weight of his bodyguards pressing against him at Sabha as he frantically tried to disenchant the djinn before it could rip them apart.

I won't be helpless, Khalid decided, and oscillated to mage sight before he could think the better of it.

The room was suffused with color. Reds, ambers, and vibrant greens twined around thick ropes of blue and copper. The twisting patterns of yellowed silver slipped into a neon frenzy of violet and gold. Khalid couldn't breathe.

The patterns were too rich. The air tasted like blood mixed with honey: rotten and ripe. It was glorious and hideous; pain and pleasure joined into an ecstatic union. Khalid tried to inhale, but the heavy magick crushed his chest like a stone.

Then he saw it: an ice-blue sliver of a spell shaking against the weight of the Oracle's prediction, picking it apart. Khalid could see Zephyr's spell but didn't have the skill to help; the pattern was far too intricate. He was as helpless as a mundane.

But as vulnerable as a mage.

The magick stroked his skin, squeezing until Khalid dropped his shields. It rushed into his personal power. His vision swam, and he hung suspended in a blur of reverberating magick that sung across his eardrums.

The Oracle was still prophesizing images of destruction, but he couldn't see them. There was no future, no past, only the here and now. Khalid lost himself in the fragrance of jasmine and the taste of oranges.

The cold wind lifted his hair. Instead of coming to his senses, Khalid fell prey to the delicious lick of ice across his overheated neck. Now he knew what it meant to feel alive!

His aura pulsed with the power pressing against him, and all at once, the gibberish of the Oracle's mimed spells made sense. Such a simple explanation for why his constructs didn't live! His djinn spells were too elegant, too perfectly drawn. Spells to create life, to fuse possibility into reality, had to be as messy and incoherent as life itself.

Without thinking, Khalid started to cast. It was almost impossible *not* to cast, there was so much magick in the room. And all of it pooled into him: the pivot point in an unwanted, unavoidable future.

He started with a simple three-turn, but instead of methodically layering the spell patterns atop that foundation, he meandered through the djinn enchantment. He added a herringbone wash just because it was pretty. An arabesque bracket that flipped into an inner rocker. He didn't incorporate any instructions into the design. He didn't limit or restrict his construct. He just bent the wind.

How effortless it was! Khalid released the spell, and wondered how many djinni he might create before the magick running thick in this cave gave out. He was so energized, he could cast for days. Nothing mattered except channeling the eager power awaiting *his* will, *his* vision for what must become.

Two thin, bluish hands reached through the patterns, and a silver-haired djinn emerged. His whirlwind ripped Pythia's paper from her easel, spinning it into a shower of confetti. It would have lifted Pythia up as well, but she clung tightly to the wooden frame bolted to the floor. Khalid clung to his seat, marveling that this djinn didn't bear his likeness.

The construct twisted around the room, his lower half spinning so fast it scoured the limestone and shook the mirrors. Dust and grit blew into Khalid's face.

Khalid blinked rapidly, his eyes tearing. The powdered stone coated his hair like the bloody sand that covered him at Sabha, and terror pushed away the power-drunk exuberance that had captured him. He closed his eyes.

The taste of fruit and wine vanished, though a patina of magick still glowed through his eyelids. Sparks of light flickered as if his retinas had been sun-damaged. He exhaled slowly and tried to remember where he was. Why he was here.

"You can dance!" Eurus's delighted voice whipped around the room, louder than the crackle of the djinn's lightning.

Khalid opened his eyes, this time careful to keep his vision limited to the mundane spectrum.

Eurus had manifested, her white hands clasped around the djinn's larger blue forearms as they spun in a circle around the room. They twisted through the images of devastation cast by the Oracle without care, laughing. The gale force of their passage plastered Khalid to his seat, but somehow the three mages were completely unaffected. Not even their veils fluttered.

Zephyr's reflected face was furrowed in concentration, and he had not shifted his stiff stance. The elemental was still casting, still fighting the fate that Khalid refused to believe would be unchangeable.

A crack rang out. Zephyr's mouth opened in astonishment.

Fighting the gusts of wind that pinned him to his seat, Khalid whipped his head toward the sound. Pythia held a parabolic pistol, her sights set on Zephyr. She fired again, but the elemental dematerialized.

"No!" Eurus's scream ricocheted around the cave. The gale force gusts stopped abruptly, and Khalid fell out of his chair in the sudden absence of countervailing pressure.

Pythia's second shot had passed through the empty air where Zephyr had stood, striking the newborn djinn. Eurus floated over his prone form, her white hands stained a purplish-blue as she pressed them against his chest. The djinn closed his eyes.

Khalid leapt from the floor and grabbed Pythia's pistol from her hands. She didn't try to resist, but he wasn't taking any chances. He pulled her around, cocking the Luger to load another round into the chamber before pressing it against the side of her head.

But he didn't shoot.

He didn't know what role the mundane officiant played in a prophecy. Perhaps, like the petitioner, her presence was required for the spell to work. Khalid held her tightly as he scanned the room for other threats.

The Oracle hadn't moved, and their images of violence, death, and emptiness continued to flood the suddenly-still room in technicolor. The passing seconds felt like hours as he tried to decide what to do.

"No one can change a fated future, Amir," Pythia said, her voice hoarse.

"Since when do you come to a ritual armed with a pistol and iron bullets?" Khalid countered, pressing the barrel harder against her skull.

"We've been preparing for this moment since the Oracle first prophesized that the winds would return to contend against Fate."

The devotees, at least, knew how to use a prophecy.

"I failed," Eurus cried. Her voice careened around the cavern while she hovered over the fallen djinn.

"Where is Zephyr now?" Khalid asked.

The elemental simply stared at the blue blood dripping off her hands. They didn't have time for Eurus to have a meltdown. Khalid repeated his question, more sharply this time.

"Casting." Eurus didn't look up from the djinn.

"But it's harder to cast complex spells when you're disembodied," Khalid said, recalling what Zephyr had told him before they entered the cave.

Eurus nodded. "I was supposed to guard him. I got distracted."

"Help him," Khalid urged. "Share your power. Do whatever it takes! This prophecy cannot come to pass."

"Are you prepared to die to prevent it?" Pythia demanded.

Khalid tightened his grip, but the senior devotee wasn't dissuaded.

"Prepared to sacrifice your magick, your life, your lands? Great magick requires great sacrifice!"

He refused to let her rattle him. "Eurus!" Khalid called.

The faerie finally looked up at him.

He held her gaze for a moment. "Help Zephyr."

She nodded, fading into the air. At the same time, Zephyr's gray face reappeared, slowly followed by the rest of his body. He hovered over the robe Pythia had lent him, concentrating on the spell he was still trying to cast.

Khalid watched him for a moment, thinking. Even if he dared oscillate his sight, he still wasn't sure how to help. Zephyr's spell was far beyond his skill, even if this ritual was flooding him with enough power to perform the impossible.

"What's left for you to do, now?" Khalid asked Pythia. "Your paper is gone. Is your sketching necessary to finish the ritual?"

"No," Pythia said. "Only my presence is required."

Good, Khalid thought. He pulled the pistol back and cuffed her on the side of the head. Her body crumpled, and he let her fall.

He put the pistol down on the easel's shelf and braced himself. He didn't usually take a battlemage's "casting stance," but none of his usual enchantments would help. There was only one spell he might cast that could, but he couldn't allow himself to be overcome by the sensation of Delphi's magick again.

All great magicks run in threes. The truism made more sense now. Zephyr and Eurus needed a third to help them. If he could control himself, he could be that third.

He took a moment to stare at the Oracle's prophetic vision. His guaranteed victory was an empty annihilation. A world gone extinct, emptied of life. And yet, he'd lived through one apocalypse already. Khalid forced himself to open to the memory: the messy horror of blood-soaked sand, the feel of blood-soaked robes clinging to his legs, the rotten scent of mutilated bodies baking in the desert sun.

He needed to hold onto that horror so the cave's magick couldn't turn his senses.

Khalid inhaled and shifted his sight.

The magick roared up, and he struggled to find the ice-blue lines of Zephyr's spell. Interfering in an active casting was dangerous, but he had no choice. He needed to bind himself to Zephyr, to give the faerie his unwanted power. The Oracle had already given voice to their prophecy. Once the released magick completed its rush to the pivot point, their prophetic spell would be complete.

He was supposed to be the spell's outlet, a lightning rod for the power of possibility that had been harnessed into an inescapable fate. The magick desired him almost as much as he desired it. The lush ecstasy popping into his personal power was overwhelming.

Blood, Khalid reminded himself. *The smell of blood.* He could resist the allure. He could. Khalid started to cast. It was a gamble, but he hoped with the power of a pivot, Zephyr would succeed.

The binding spell was too easy, too simplistic. A serpentine loop with a backward-flowing motif. It took no time at all to create a central conduit to his personal power and open it to Zephyr.

The faerie didn't hesitate. He pulled hard, drawing Khalid's power to him with sharp tugs. It was as though Zephyr were being forced to sip through a straw when he needed to gulp.

Khalid's heart stuttered, and he dropped to the ground beside Pythia. Between Zephyr's slow draining of his personal power and the flood of new magick entering his aura, he wasn't sure he could remain conscious long enough to finish what he'd started.

Great magick requires great sacrifice.

That truism lingered in his mind. Khalid struggled to

keep his eyes open while pushing all his power outward through the central line of his new binding.

An eternity passed as Khalid trembled with the strain of keeping his eyes open while letting go of his power. Not even the wind made noise anymore. Sweat beaded Zephyr's brow, and Khalid felt clammy with perspiration. He was going into shock. But he'd honed his endurance by casting so many djinni. He wouldn't pass out, wouldn't let his body instinctively reclaim the power that Zephyr needed.

The ice-blue lines had grown into a near-incandescent mass. If there was a pattern, Khalid didn't recognize it.

At least he was only gambling with his own life now. And if he died, then this prophecy would have to fade back into a mere prognostication. The image of one likely, though not inescapable, future.

Khalid pressed his magick outward again, flooding Zephyr with even more power than the Oracle's prophecy was sending him. He was bleeding himself dry so that the elemental's spell might succeed. He no longer felt anything. All his senses had been compressed into his sight. The magick pulsed through his eyes like a heartbeat.

"*Beware!*" The Oracle's voice echoed. All three jerked upright as if they'd been plucked from their supine positions by an invisible hand. "*The ties that bind!*"

The overlapping colors and textures coating the room contracted into a congealed mass that exploded outward with their speech. The magick had been transformed into a multicolored mural coiled over the cavern's walls.

The mages dropped as if the strings holding them up had been cut. A part of him wondered if they were dead now, all used up in this misbegotten rite of prophecy.

Khalid himself was bereft. Empty and cold, lying on stone that had been swept clean by his now-dead djinn. It was smooth like twice-milled silk beneath his hand. The floor felt like his only friend. He closed his eyes.

"I did it!" Zephyr's exultant tone seemed far away. "I battled fate and won!"

"Not fair," Eurus's voice hung in the air.

Khalid didn't have the energy to look.

"We promised the worst that would happen would be that he would leave here with a prophecy."

"And so he will, 'The ties that bind,'" Zephyr quoted. "Not as glorious a future as the victory the Oracle first prophesized, but more useful perhaps to his current struggle."

"He has given more than he received," Eurus said. "It's not *fair*."

Zephyr didn't respond, and Khalid found the silence restful. The fae were obsessed with fairness. He needed peace. What did fair matter now?

"This cannot be *his* sacrifice," Eurus continued.

She sounded furious. He'd never heard that tone in her voice before.

Khalid tried to find the will to open his eyes when a slow nudge tripped across his senses. First, he felt a tickle in his feet, then pins and needles as his numbness evaporated.

He opened one eye to see Zephyr funneling power into his aura. The swirl of color and texture intensified into such sharp pain, it forced both his eyes wide open. Khalid screamed until he had no voice left.

Then it was over. He felt — himself.

He blinked rapidly, shifting his sight from mage to mundane and back. The magick released by the redirected prophecy was still there, a rich flow of iridescent sparks, but it wasn't seeking him out.

He marveled that he had the energy to sit up. And when he'd managed that, he decided he might as well try standing. He staggered to his feet, deliberately avoiding the sight of the wind elementals as he pivoted slowly to examine the new mural magically etched into the wall.

It was still a scene of war, which didn't surprise him: war seemed to be all he knew. But this war, at least, was different from the images the Oracle had first shown him. The aeroplanes were different, and the sky wasn't filled with clouds of fire. Khalid stared at the image of a fat, waxy-leaved bush covered in sharp needles protruding from the sand. Nothing like that grew in Arabia.

He was giddy with relief. *Even if I can't break free of war, at least I won't destroy my own deserts.*

With that hopeful thought, Khalid managed to look at the two elementals. Eurus had her head cocked to one side as she examined her brother. Her hand reached out to stroke his shoulder, clean and white.

The image of that hand dripping with blue blood flashed through Khalid's mind, and he glanced at his fallen djinn. So odd to think that he'd actually managed to create life, even one so short-lived. He couldn't remember how he'd done it. If the proof of his success didn't lie there, he would have thought it a dream of omnipotence brought on by excess magick consumption.

"This sacrifice is not fair!" Zephyr's voice shuttled around the room. "How do they endure their confinement?"

Khalid turned to look at him. The elemental's gray skin used to shine like polished metal, but now it was dull, as if its luster had been rubbed out.

"This is something new," Eurus said in an upbeat tone.

Zephyr blinked rapidly.

Khalid swallowed hard when he saw the elemental's ice-blue irises, each with a pinpoint pupil floating within them.

Zephyr's newly-made eyes stared into his own. If Khalid thought the elemental's appearance before was frightening, this near-human look was worse.

"Two more prophecies must be spoken," Eurus said, examining the mural. "Then I'll find the three pivots and use their power to pull you back into air. In the meantime, you should enjoy the novelty of this experience."

"Novelty?" Zephyr huffed, his outraged voice ricocheting around the room.

Eurus ignored her brother's outburst, turning instead to look directly at Khalid, her angular face somehow soft. "Don't worry. You're not the pivot of this new prophecy. But Zephyr's sacrifice has given you a bit more capacity than you had before."

She bent down to examine the senior devotee. "Pythia was correct in one thing. The prophecy has indeed gone awry. It will ricochet around until it finds a suitable outlet."

Eurus stood, and a gust of wind blew Pythia into a seated position against the wall. The East Wind smiled at Khalid. "I've kept my promise all the same. Once you've recovered from today's exertions, you'll see that your personal power is even greater than it was before. Fair is fair."

Khalid glanced at the binding that still linked him to Zephyr. A gust of wind rifled the elemental's hair.

"Oh, very well!" Zephyr said. "Fair is fair."

Khalid felt a final tug as Zephyr unraveled the spell, and inhaled with relief as his aura settled around him, free of the invasive bond.

"That's settled then," Eurus declared. "Bravo, Brother! You have indeed broken the future. I'll be back soon to check on you. Don't look so glum. This is *new!*"

She dissolved into air, and the sharp breeze ruffled Khalid's robe. He bent down and picked up Pythia's cloak.

He shook it out, and an iron bullet clattered to the floor, rolling until it encountered the unconscious devotee herself.

Zephyr hadn't broken the future. Not really. He'd just set it free.

"Here," Khalid offered the cloak to the faerie, whose gray skin had puckered in goosebumps. He wondered if Zephyr was now mortal or just unable to merge with the air.

When Zephyr didn't move to take it, Khalid stepped closer to the former elemental, draping it over his shoulders.

Zephyr startled at the touch, blinking rapidly before he fastened it closed.

"Is it very different?" Khalid asked.

"Unimaginably so," Zephyr replied.

Khalid was getting more used to his misplaced voice.

"Shall we?" Khalid gestured to the opening.

Zephyr glided forward, and Khalid was glad to see him hovering a few inches above the floor. The elemental might have been un-magicked in some way, but he was still a wind faerie.

"Perhaps with time, I will find some pleasure in this prison of flesh." Zephyr paused at the base of the stairs.

"Your offspring do," Khalid replied.

"True," Zephyr said and really looked at him.

Khalid forced himself to maintain eye contact.

"Don't give up your experiments," Zephyr said. "Even if your desert doesn't hold the same power of possibility as this place. Keep trying to make your djinni live. Eurus clings to the hope that you can do it. Everyone needs hope."

"Everyone needs hope," Khalid repeated softly. That was the truth.

DJINN SWARM

1

RIYADH, ARABIA. PRESENT DAY

AMIR KHALID'S forehead furrowed in concentration as he considered the three bottles of ambrosia his aide had brought up from the palace cellars. The soft swirl of compressed magick glittered within the heavy glass bottles. The 1968 shone with its characteristic pure-gold color, but the room's dim light wasn't strong enough to bring out its true magnificence.

Khalid flicked his ringed finger at the sitting room window, activating the palace household spells. The shutters opened another fifteen degrees. Now, the ambrosia's color boiled with its trademark rainbow luminescence.

But the 1968 Jubbah XO Select was only special because it was so old, and therefore exceedingly rare. This century's advances in skimming and refinement technologies had dramatically improved the flavor of Arabian ambrosia. So the 1968 was only really suitable for display, and Khalid wanted to give his treasured guest something to savor.

"Not the '68," Khalid told his aide, wondering why he was making this so hard. He didn't actually need to give her a bottle of ambrosia. She was only expecting a ring to control the palace's household spells.

"The 2007, then?" the aide asked, putting the rejected bottle back in the padded case.

"Let me see the rings first," Khalid replied curtly, irritated at his man's presumption. Of course the 2007 would be the proper choice, but Khalid wasn't going through the trouble of personally selecting a gift to simply follow protocol.

The aide raised an eyebrow but otherwise didn't comment. He inclined his head before leaving Khalid's suite to gather a selection of rings from the palace magesmith.

The were-jaguar at the door wasn't as circumspect as Khalid's aide. "You are paying more attention to this American doctor than your research." Fernanda's Spanish accent softened her words, but her tone was sharper than ever.

"Don't you have more important things to do than guard my door?" Khalid demanded.

Fernanda shrugged. "The Americans are important."

"Then maybe you should be watching them instead of me."

"And maybe you should consider why you obsess over her. It's not like you, Amir." With that, Fernanda left as swiftly and silently as all jaguars.

Khalid stared at the door, struck by her stiletto thrust of an exit line. Even when the were-jaguars weren't killing mages, they could still do damage. Since the weres typically took cat form while in the private wing of the palace, Fernanda's decision to remain human meant she'd intended to say something to him today.

She was right about one thing: the Americans were important. *And dangerous*, he reminded himself. This state visit was the first time any American had been allowed into the country since their government had funded his late nephew Hisham's rebellion a decade ago. If it weren't for the American doctor's remarkable success with the procedure to restore mage-sight, they'd be forbidden entry for at least another decade.

Keeping the doctor happy until she operated on Loujain was essential. That had to be the reason his younger sister was flirting with her so much. It was certainly the reason Khalid was personally selecting a suitable gift for her. He looked at the two bottles on the table. In this light, the 2011's sunset color looked practically red, while the 2007 gleamed with the gold promise of the noonday sun.

Khalid reached for the 2007 but hesitated.

This shouldn't be a difficult decision. The 2007 was more than acceptable. The silica-salt had been skimmed from his own fields in the Empty Quarter, making this a personal gift. He'd sent two bottles of the 2007 to the Danjou Enclave elders, so giving her the same ambrosia would indicate he saw her as an equivalent power. Moreover, experts considered this particular vintage to be among the finest ever brewed!

He didn't know why he'd asked his aide to bring up the ice-brewed 2011. Ambrosia connoisseurs found the bloody color of all 2011s off-putting. Even casual consumers knew that year's silica-salt had been ruined.

Khalid picked up the bottle anyway. The red-gold liquid sparkled with compressed power. He sighed. For most of 2011, Khalid's djinni had crisscrossed Arabia's silica-salt fields searching for traitors hiding in the desert. That year's ambrosia might pack more of a power punch than any other vintage, but its rancid flavor made it practically undrinkable.

He turned the bottle so that the ambrosia swirled with flashes of gold and bright red. Maybe if he wrote an accompanying note. *It's not a sunset, it's a sunrise,* he would say. *The taint of war can be healed, the damage overcome.*

But his mind blanked when he tried to come up with more words to explain why this ambrosia was so special. Without context, she'd wonder why he was giving her a vintage the experts considered too contaminated with spell residue to even taste.

Other tribes had unloaded their spoiled brews at rock-bottom prices. The residue rendered them unsuitable as an elixir base, and their acrid taste unacceptable as sipping ambrosia. But Khalid had kept every bottle from his fields. *Waste not, want not,* his mother used to say. And there had certainly been times when he'd been desperate enough to swallow rotgut ambrosia.

But he wasn't desperate anymore. Even when he had to cast djinn spells night after night to hunt down all the traitors, he'd had high-quality ambrosia to fuel his spellcasting. It took five years before Khalid had any reason to open a 2011.

Crushing the American-funded rebellion had come at the bitter price of destroying their brother's line down four generations. There had been nothing for al-Saaqib to celebrate and much to mourn. But a symbolic toast was necessary the day he and his sisters invited their niece Hamida to resurrect the House of Hassan and join their ruling Quatrone.

Loujain had flown the four of them into the heart of the desert, deep within the Empty Quarter. Newly returned to the House of Hassan after her contract marriage ended, Hamida must have wondered whether she was going to be executed like everyone else in her line. Her stoic expression softened with surprise when they instead asked her to restore their brother's house. Khalid had uncorked the bottle. Faiza made a rather cold toast. Then the four of them pounded the first glass as if it were a shot.

They were all expecting the bitter flavor of betrayal, a reminder of how their last ruling Quatrone had fallen apart. Instead, they were greeted with the taste of candied citrus balanced with a complex floral finish. The vintage's near-perfect balance of power and purity had felt like a symbol of what their newly reconstituted Quatrone could be.

Now, Khalid opened the bottles during special family celebrations: weddings and the like. In his workroom, he'd stashed a left-over quarter-bottle in case he needed a boost to get through a difficult casting.

He put the ambrosia back on the table. They couldn't risk offending the doctor before she cured Loujain. He should just give her the 2007 and be done with it. He started to reach for the 2007, but picked up the 2011 again. He flicked his ring at the blinds, angling his hand until only a faint sliver of sunlight illuminated the room. Dull glints of gold hinted at the incredible power contained within the liquid.

I'll present it to her in person, he decided. Bring his open bottle so she could taste how different this particular vintage was from other 2011s. She'd decline at first, of course. The doctor was cautious. But then, he'd explain that this ambrosia had been ice-brewed, a rare method of refinement that neutralized the impact of external spells and enchantments on the raw silica-salt.

How he longed to see her expression when she experienced it. Her face would soften with surprise. Then he could explain how this ambrosia represented the Saaqib tribe's restart, the healing of the rift that had begun when his nephew used American funding to finance his uprising.

Khalid put the bottle down abruptly. Fernanda was right. He was coming up with ridiculous excuses to see the

American. Despite the importance of her visit, no one — and especially not Doctor Amy Elizabeth Bant — expected him to devote his personal attention to her.

The thought of Amy's name sent an electrifying tingle across his skin as if he'd tasted the drink he planned to give her. *Enough of this,* Khalid scolded himself.

The outer door to his apartment chimed, and Khalid used a sharp gesture to activate the opening spell. His aide entered, followed by Julio, one of Fernanda's more senior were-jaguars.

Fernanda led her mercenary clan of were-jaguars fearlessly, but she wasn't stupid enough to tempt his temper. She'd pushed his boundaries with her parting gibe. *Deliberately,* Khalid thought. Fernanda did nothing without purpose. Before he could consider that further, his aide placed the velvet-lined tray on the table in front of Khalid.

"Depending on which finger she prefers, the magesmith believes these will be suitable."

Khalid nodded at the bottles on the table. "The doctor who restores Loujain's sight deserves more than we gave the American elders. Calibrate two gift boxes for thirteen degrees. Put the 2011 in gold leaf and the 2007 in silver."

"Yes, Al-Amir," the man replied and began packing them up.

Khalid frowned in concentration as he picked up one enchanted ring after another.

"Should I bring another set?" His aide's tone was respectful, but his impatience showed. Khalid never bothered with such questions of gifts, décor, or even his own clothing. Those were matters he delegated to his spouses or advisors.

But this was different. Doctor Amy was important.

Khalid studied the options. All of them were far too

gaudy for the doctor, whose sole ornamentation appeared to be her brilliant-white lab coat.

"Have the mage-smith send over anything that can be sized to fit," Khalid told him.

The aide bowed and left, but the were-jaguar didn't follow him.

"You can go," Khalid told him.

"Fernanda wants us to remain within striking distance until we discover which of the Americans are spies," Julio replied.

"All of them are," Khalid said. *Except her,* he thought, picking up a ring at random.

His mouth quirked up in a slight smile as he remembered her belated compliments when she tasted the dishes served at the welcome banquet. Her sister's husband, the truth-teller, hadn't flinched at her bland remarks. But his careful expression at the American ambassador's effusive compliments spoke volumes. Doctor Amy Elizabeth Bant was too honest to be a spy. *Amy,* he thought, and a shiver of pleasure tripped across his skin.

He frowned and tried to regain his focus.

"Until the Americans leave, four of us will be in the private wing," Julio said.

"It would be easier to catch the spies if you gave them an opening," Khalid said. "I'm more than capable of defending myself."

"Usually," Julio replied.

Now Khalid was annoyed. "Wait outside," he ordered.

"I'll be just outside your door," Julio said, striding out with a jaguar's insouciant grace.

Khalid had to content himself with that compromise. He wondered if Amy's were-guards were as outspoken and independent as his own.

A rainbow of light glinted off the diamond ring he held, reminding him of her. Amy glowed as hot as the sun, with a pivot's power to make her skin shine with an inner radiance.

But it wasn't her obvious strength as a mage that made her special. It was her skill as a mundane doctor. *And that is the reason I must keep her happy,* Khalid told himself. Without Amy's help, Loujain would never regain her sight.

Which had to be the reason Loujain was so focused on pleasing her. She'd even brought Doctor Amy to their tribal meal! If Khalid had so boldly breached centuries of custom and tradition, their older sister Faiza would have taken him to task. But they both indulged Loujain.

Really, it was Loujain who was paying undue attention to their treasured guest. The were-jaguars should be cautioning her, not him! Loujain was behaving like a character in one of Cairo's never-ending stream of forgettable romance movies: the beautiful and rich patient who falls for the aloof and brilliant doctor.

If his little sister didn't back off, he'd have to put her in her place.

Khalid put the ring down abruptly.

What's the matter with me? He was usually relieved when his sister took on such duties. Until now, his greatest wish was to have the freedom to work uncomplicated by anyone's attention.

How ironic that Doctor Amy wanted that as well. She'd told him she needed to focus on treating his sister, that she couldn't allow herself to think about anything other than her work. Which is what he, of course, should desire above all else, too. They'd brought her here — allowed the Americans back into their country — for one reason only: to save Loujain's life.

But when Khalid considered how charming his little sister was, how passionate, how charismatic, he didn't want to wait until her lack of mage-sight killed her. He wanted to kill her himself.

Khalid stood up and strode to the window, adjusting the shades manually until the room flooded with sunlight. Waves of purple, silver, and umber ambient magick coated the walls. It was an unfamiliar agony, thinking about how easily Loujain captured the hearts of anyone she wanted. He watched the play of magick in the room until his pulse stopped pounding.

Loujain could try seduction, but Doctor Amy was the consummate professional. She was too like him to be beguiled by his little sister's irrepressible charm. The doctor clung to her mundane medical ethics. She wouldn't allow her patient to romance her any more than she'd allow her patient's brother to do the same.

Khalid sighed. He should back off, allow her to do her job and leave. But the thought of Amy leaving was so painful, he couldn't quite hold onto it. Instead, he imagined bringing her the promised ring tonight. He'd wait until dinnertime, after she had lingered far too late in her office. He couldn't allow their treasured guest to go without sustenance, he'd tell her. And then he could bring her to his private garden and serve her himself.

He couldn't shake the look of her! The way her blond hair seemed to capture the sunlight, the glittery luminescence of her pale face. She could be a wind faerie, she was so pale. But for all her power, her skin had lost its elasticity: she wasn't casting the spells for constant cell regeneration.

He could teach her.

Or offer to teach her. Surely that would be reason enough to—

"What now?" Khalid asked. His aide had returned with three more trays.

"Perhaps one of these will be acceptable," the man murmured, setting the trays out on the table.

"Leave them. I'll call for you."

"Al-Amir, the mage-smith will need time to adjust them," his aide remarked.

Khalid sighed. The man wouldn't leave until he made a decision.

"Very well." Khalid sat back down at the table, glancing over the selection. There were too many. This was why he never bothered with these matters himself. But no one else knew the doctor well enough to make such a choice.

After a moment, Khalid picked up a ring set with a sapphire cabochon. There was a mystery in such a setting: while the stone looked lifeless and dull to mundane-sight, the style allowed the elegance of the enchantment to sparkle without competition. *Amy might like this*, Khalid mused. *Protocol will be satisfied with the 2007 ambrosia, so I can afford to please her with a stone most would consider lesser.*

"This one," Khalid said, handing the sapphire ring to his aide. "Have the smith approximate the sizing for her forefinger."

"Everything will be delivered before dinner," his man answered, and started to pick up the gift boxes.

"Leave those," Khalid said. "Bring the ring back when it's ready. I'll present them to her myself."

His aide avoided eye contact as he stacked the trays. "Yes, Al-Amir," he murmured, bowing again before he left.

Khalid frowned as he stared at the two boxes of ambrosia on the table. He pushed his chair back and stood up. Fernanda was right. He had *never* felt like this before. And he had known many beautiful mages, mages whose skin sparkled almost as brightly as Amy's. None of them had sparked his interest, let alone consumed his every thought.

This distraction wasn't normal. He tried to remember whether he'd checked himself for invasive spells this morning, but couldn't even recall casting his own daily spells. He might not remember to eat while preoccupied with a new spell design, but he *always* remembered what spells he cast.

Khalid prided himself on the care he took in spellcraft and battle preparations alike. Certainly, his late nephew's American-funded rebellion had taught them all the value of self-care. Since barely escaping that assassination attempt, he had been diligent about conducting a daily personal spell check.

Except he didn't remember checking himself today.

He'd been so preoccupied at breakfast that he hadn't even noticed Faiza's evaluation of him for hidden spells. His sister's presumption should have provoked a reaction, but it had taken Fernanda's sharp comments to shake him from his stupor.

It could be a love spell, Khalid thought dutifully, though he couldn't quite believe the honest doctor would do such a thing, even if he could imagine she had the skill to cast it. Still, enclave mages, especially American enclave mages like the visiting Danjou, had no morals. One of her advisors could have done it without her knowledge.

For some reason, Khalid hesitated. *Who cares if it's a spell?* That thought terrified him enough that he hurried into his workroom for the first time since the American delegation had arrived.

The unfinished, multicolored diagram of his latest work-in-progress covered the whiteboard, but he had no interest in fiddling with it now. He pressed the button on the wall. As the whiteboard lifted up on its track, exposing the floor-length mirror behind it, he flipped the blind dial to open the window coverings to twenty-seven percent.

He oscillated his vision to mage-sight and considered

the quality of the light in the room for spell-evaluation. *A bit too bright,* he thought, turning the dial down to twenty-two. The rhythm of such preparations helped Khalid calm down.

He was approaching this problem as methodically as he did everything else, which undercut the notion that he was under the influence of a love spell. But even Faiza had noticed his preoccupation, and Fernanda had told him outright that he was behaving erratically.

He wasn't behaving normally because he didn't feel normal. As observant as the jaguars were, they couldn't read minds, and what they were noticing was but a tiny sliver of the intense interest he had in the American doctor.

It has to be a spell, he told himself.

Khalid unbuttoned his robe. The various spells on his garments might obscure other enchantments — perhaps even one more devious than his late nephew's mages had cast. Faiza could have missed it this morning. And if he was too distracted to notice her poking into his personal power, maybe he'd been too distracted during his previous morning ablutions.

He stripped completely, tossing his clothes into a heap beside the counter. Naked, Khalid stepped in front of the mirror and considered the teal and gray cloud that swirled around his reflection. His aura was robust, vibrant. He didn't use many personal via-enchantments — he had no talent for spelling living things — but there were two that he wore every day.

Khalid pulled the dampening enchantment out from his skin and dissolved it. After his trip to the Oracle's caves, he'd begun casting it to hide the increase in his personal power. Without the dampener, his aura flexed outward in a glistening peacock display until he shone with a corona of pure magick.

It was odd to stare at his reflection like this. *Vanity, thy name is mage,* he scolded himself, but didn't stop looking. Most mages found such displays of personal power attractive; Khalid knew he was unusual in his typical indifference. His mind flittered toward Amy's pastel-soaked skin, and his cock jumped.

He ought to pull his other spell from his skin to see if anything were hiding beneath it. But instead, Khalid found himself staring at the swirl of his personal power, wondering if Amy found him at all appealing.

He oscillated his sight to the mundane spectrum. Right now, he'd calibrated his look at around thirty — a little older than most mages chose, but it helped with the mundanes, who still had a hard time accepting authority in a youthful package. He could adjust his constant cell regeneration spell to age up or down if she preferred older or younger men.

He pulled the via-enchantment to the surface of his skin, where it sparkled like a glittery pink tattoo. His skin was darker than hers, but he hoped the magick that lit it from within would appeal to her. He was clean-shaven, but could grow a beard if she preferred that. *Should I ask her?* Khalid was sure that would be too forward for the reserved doctor.

Khalid shook his head. *I'm a fool,* he thought. He knew what obsession felt like. He'd obsessed over the construction of the djinn spell for years, his work constantly on the edge of his mind as he focused single-mindedly on crafting the spell that had won his tribe dominion over the Arabian and Saharan deserts.

But his obsession with his research hadn't resulted in this kind of physiological reaction. Even thinking about her caused his blood to surge. And the pounding of his pulse wasn't helping his concentration. He should want to purge such an utterly frivolous feeling. No good could come of this yearning for an American doctor. And why would he enjoy feeling this sense of a bowstring drawn taut every time he thought about seeing her again?

But there was an insidious pleasure in the flush of heat that rolled through him when she appeared. And the sheer delight of her smile made him want to touch her.

Even if these sensations had no good reason to erupt, and even if his elder sister was right — that heartbreak was worse than the fleeting joy of desire — he didn't want to let the feeling go.

The glittery pink lines of the constant cell regeneration spell fluttered along his torso, reminding him of how his traitorous nephew Hisham's via-enchanter had almost killed him. Only Khalid's battlefield habit of conducting a daily spellcheck had saved him.

Enough, Khalid told himself, pulling his cell regeneration spell completely out of his skin. The orange-shaded pink whirls flickered at the very edge of his aura. He rippled through his schemas as he searched his body for anything else.

Nothing. He saw nothing. Nothing cast on his own skin, no extra layers of spellwork tacked onto his personal via-enchantment. Khalid was relieved to realize that, whatever his odd feeling for the doctor was, it didn't come from a spell.

But as he was about to turn away, he saw a slight shadow running along the outer edge of the cell regeneration spell. His stomach clenched.

No, he told himself. *Hijacking a regeneration spell is more trouble than it's worth.* His heart pounded as he stared at his reflection. The constant cell regeneration spell only lasted twenty-to-thirty hours and had to be recast daily. He'd only cast this via-enchantment when he woke up today —

yet he hadn't stopped thinking about her since she'd arrived.

Khalid narrowed his eyes to focus on the blip in the pattern. *Just an unfinished three-turn,* he was relieved to realize. There was no trace of anyone else's magick.

He recast the enchantment, feeling the slight pucker along the edge of his arm as his now-perfect spell settled into his bones. He'd been focusing so much on tweaking the regeneration spells for Loujain, he'd grown lax in his personal spelling.

Or distracted by *her.*

He shook his head at his reflection before picking up his clothes and getting dressed. *I'm not going to recast the dampener spell,* he thought, giddy with the confidence that his new passion wasn't another American plot.

It was ridiculous, but hadn't he earned a chance to be ridiculous? He'd freed Arabia from the Magi, evicted the Europeans from the Sahara, dutifully cared for his sisters as himself. He hadn't flinched at executing his brother's traitorous heir, eradicating four generations of his brother's house.

Khalid pulled his open bottle of 2011 ice-brewed ambrosia from the mini-fridge. It wouldn't take much longer for the mage-smith to resize the ring, and then he could discover whether Amy could ignore his unrestrained appearance as easily as she'd shrugged him off before.

The outer doorbell chimed. Khalid tapped his ring to open the door to his apartment. His aides would likely be relieved to see him back in his workroom again.

Khalid adjusted the collar on his tunic, frowning slightly at his reflection. He should change into the green and gold one before meeting the doctor. His spouses always said green made his skin sparkle.

"Al-Amir."

Khalid turned, surprised to hear Prime Minister Malik's voice. His friend's face was grim.

"What's wrong?" Khalid asked.

Malik's heavy black eyebrow raised. "Am I that obvious? I'd hoped to hide my concern from the Americans."

"Which Americans?" Khalid's voice was sharper than it should be.

"The changeling truth-teller," Malik replied. "I'm going to need your help."

2

RIYADH, ARABIA

MIKE STOOD with Ambassador Godfrey in the embassy's rooftop receiving room, waiting for the palace carpets to arrive. As a lifelong diplomat, the ambassador had a good poker face, but Mike was a trained observer. Godfrey was anxious.

"Amira Hamida offered to give me a private tour of the al-Saaqib refinement facility and silica-salt fields," Ambassador Godfrey said. "But I'm not sure how this fits into their agenda. That's why I want you to tag along. The only American the Quatrone cares about is Doctor Bant, and since Arabs consider siblings practically the same person, your mere presence should help this outing go smoothly." *Truth.*

"I'm Amy's brother-in-law," Mike felt compelled to clarify. "Not her actual brother."

Godfrey waved off his objection. "To them, it's the same. You're Amy's brother as long as you're married to her sister. These Arabs really seem to believe siblings are one person in multiple bodies, so if you're with me, I won't have to worry about being abandoned in the desert." *Exaggeration.*

Mike swallowed at the overripe flavor of the ambassador's hyperbole. Godfrey was expecting mere diplomatic danger, not an assassination attempt.

"Besides," Ambassador Godfrey continued. "You can help me figure out whether this is just another opportunity for me to grovel for America's past sins or a different kind of thing altogether."

Godfrey was a genius at groveling, but they both knew that wouldn't be enough to get them the supplies the U.S. needed. "Amira Hamida can't see magick either, so it's unlikely they really intend to show off their refining techniques," Mike said.

The ambassador nodded. "This outing feels contrived. It could be a test of our good faith." *Truth.*

Mike appreciated Godfrey's effort to be forthright. At best, diplomatic double-speak tasted like stale bread and pickled onions, but the crystal flavor of the ambassador's truth was a refreshing palate cleanser.

"Here." Godfrey reached into his jacket pocket and handed Mike two rolls of tropical fruit lifesavers. "I know you always have some with you, but I'm sure I'll be twisting the truth this afternoon, and I'd rather you not throw up."

"I can try to find out how much the Saaqibs really believe in this 'brother's keeper' stuff," Mike offered.

Ambassador Godfrey nodded. "My gut says yes. See if your tongue agrees."

They didn't have to wait long for Amira Hamida and her entourage of bodyguards. At twelve o'clock sharp, three carpets landed. The city's inhabitants typically took a break at midday, so the skies were mostly clear of traffic. Nevertheless, it would still take over an hour to reach the Saaqib's holdings outside the city, so they'd arrive a bit past the ideal touring time.

Not that any of them were mages to appreciate the fields' beauty. Mike doubted that anyone on this expedition would see anything special in the sand dunes. It was an odd choice to send the sole mundane member of the ruling Quatrone to accompany the mundane ambassador on a silica-salt tour. Godfrey was right to wonder at the Saaqibs' motives.

Mike couldn't taste emotions in people's speech, but the Quatrone had not exactly welcomed their delegation with open arms. Apart from a few pleasantries at the banquet, neither Amiras Faiza nor Loujain had spoken with Ambassador Godfrey. And Amir Khalid had set a distinctly chilly tone in his interactions with the American diplomats. The introduction of Amira Hamida might signify a thaw, but Mike thought it was more likely that she had come to make a point.

Hamida ibn Hisham al-Saaqib was the most recent addition to the ruling Quatrone. She'd only escaped execution alongside the rest of the House of Hassan because she'd been in a contract marriage at the time of the uprising, and so hadn't legally been her father's daughter. There had been a lot of speculation about the forty-eight-year-old — not only in the U.S., but in Arabia, also.

Speculation aside, Hamira was prompt.

Ambassador Godfrey pulled his suit straight and headed toward the hovering carpets. He offered the Amira a warm greeting in Arabic that puckered Mike's mouth slightly. The marines at the door nodded at Mike but didn't follow them out. Godfrey had decided they could best demonstrate their good faith if they went without an entourage.

"Amira Hamida, you remember Michael Arnold, Doctor

Bant's brother-in-law," Godfrey said in English as Mike drew close.

Mike offered a slight bow of his head. Hamida was wearing a yellow tunic and pants embroidered in a floral pattern. The gold and white threads caught the sunlight, glinting like they'd been studded with diamonds. If he were a mage, Mike suspected he'd see the shimmer of spells entwined in the design.

Hamida's dark face crinkled in a warm smile. "Mister Arnold. I just saw your sister at breakfast. My brother and I have high hopes that the operation will be a success." *Truth.*

Last night, she'd referred to Khalid as her uncle. It was fascinating that Hamida could truthfully call Khalid both uncle and brother.

Amira Hamida invited them to settle onto her carpet, facing forward. While Mike and Godfrey had difficulty sitting cross-legged, Hamida sank down gracefully. She was accustomed, Mike supposed, to such contortions. While there were some paved roads for trucks in Arabia, most people traveled by flying carpet or on foot.

A were-jaguar guard in human form sat beside Hamida, and they set off westward. More bodyguards in both jaguar and human form rode on smaller carpets that wove around them in a flanking formation.

Ambassador Godfrey spoke passable Arabic, but Hamida's English was near-perfect.

"Most educated Arabs learn a second language," Hamida said, dismissing Godfrey's compliment.

"Having regular access to mages is a real benefit to living in such an integrated society," Godfrey replied. "I wish I could have learned Arabic via a language-transfer spell."

"Oh, I learnt English the conventional way — hence my accent," Hamida explained.

She did sound more like a British royal than an Arabian amira, Mike noted.

"It takes a highly-skilled mind mage to perform even a basic language-transfer spell," Hamida continued. "While al-Saaqib is one of the more integrated tribes, we tend to rely on conventional means to acquire new languages."

"One of the Danjou mages warned me about mind magicks," Godfrey said. "There's apparently quite a few nasty enchantments that can be slipped in by a skilled mage when they're accessing your thoughts."

Hamida nodded. "Very true. But my siblings are perceptive enough to detect any tampering." *Truth.*

"Even Amira Loujain?" Godfrey asked blandly.

Mike wondered what the ambassador was fishing for. There had to be some purpose to this.

Hamida's mouth pursed, but her voice was even. "I was thinking of Faiza and Khalid." She smiled at Mike. "Loujain is a typical battlemage. Even if your sister cures her mage-blindness, I wouldn't seek Loujain's help with anything requiring nuanced observation."

Hamida might consider Amy his sister, but the disconnect with his understanding pickled Mike's mouth. "Forgive me, Amira, but Doctor Bant is my sister-in-law. I'm only married to her sister."

Hamida shrugged. "We don't make such distinctions. And while you Americans don't use tribal names, I understand that yours is a permanent marriage."

"Mike doesn't speak for his sister or spouse the way you speak for yours," Godfrey said. "Americans — even changelings like Mike — don't have the same conception of our intimate family members as you do here."

"*I* understand how different your customs are from ours," Hamida said sharply. "But you should understand that I am one with my siblings. I do speak for them, and they speak for me." *Truth.*

The crystalline flavor of Amira Hamida's statement was more refreshing than ice-cold water, and something about the way she said it made Mike think this was the real reason for today's outing. The Quatrone had wanted them to know that Amira Hamida wasn't interested in following in her father's rebellious footsteps.

Godfrey nodded, the usual expression of diplomatic politeness erased from his now-serious face. "I'm glad to hear it."

Mike could taste just how glad Godfrey was. He knew the ambassador really wanted to secure this trade deal. It would complicate matters exponentially if Hamida had wanted to foment another uprising.

Hamida gave them a polite, meaningless smile. "Let's get out of the city before the traffic picks up."

She said something in Arabic to the pilot. The stabilizer and wind-shield spells on the carpet were so strong, Mike could only tell he had increased their speed because the city's buildings began to blur as they soared forward.

The rest of their journey was far less fraught. Godfrey and Hamida exchanged mostly truthful small-talk during the hour-long flight over rolling dunes of white sand. Heat waves shimmered, but Mike didn't see anything magical about that. There was something peaceful in the landscape's monotony, but Mike was glad when Hamida suddenly sat up and gestured to the left. Mike and Godfrey obligingly looked down at the endless sea of sand.

"This is where the fields begin," she said.

"It's too bad neither Mike nor I can see their beauty," Godfrey said

One of Hamida's eyebrows arched upward. "You don't need to see magick to appreciate their value." *Truth.*

The carpet dipped suddenly.

"It's windy today," Hamida remarked and turned around to speak to the pilot.

Mike wasn't familiar enough with Arabian weather patterns to know how common this sudden turbulence was, but despite the stabilizing spells, the pilot had to bank the carpet a few times.

"It's too windy to go further into the larger skimming fields," Hamida announced after a second consultation with the pilot. "We'll go as far as the refinery, and you can look at one of our smaller plots. Since neither of you are mages, the silica-salt processing is probably the only part of the operation you'll be able to fully appreciate." *Lie.*

Mike popped a green lifesaver in his mouth to clear the rancid flavor. He wondered if Hamida thought there was some other aspect of the silica-salt mining they'd find interesting, or if she simply thought they couldn't appreciate any of it.

After a few minutes, the pilot slowed and took the carpet lower over the rolling dunes.

They had already flown past several skimmers working the desert sand, but this was their first close look at one of the machines. The silica-salt harvesters reminded Mike somewhat of oversized combines. They had long rolling reels in the front of the operators' cabs that spiked into the desert sand. Instead of a grain tank to capture the threshed crop, the skimmers had silk nets floating behind them to contain the silica-salt.

From Hamida's description, it seemed that a lot of ambient magick was released during the skimming process, which could overwhelm mages unprepared for the impact — one reason, perhaps, that the Quatrone had not invited the American mages on this trip.

"The primary processing facility is over there," Hamida pointed as the carpet banked in that direction.

Mike could make out shimmering waves of heat rising off a rectangular grayish square in the distance.

"It's smaller than the major plants in the Sahara," Hamida continued. "But its output is almost as great as the Sebha Refinery. Modern equipment is significantly more efficient." *Truth.*

Godfrey pointed at the building they were approaching. "The refinery appears to be made of stone. Even the roof."

Hamida provided a history of what was apparently the oldest manufacturing facility still in operation. Had she not told them, Mike never would have guessed that the front part of the building was over a thousand years old.

"We don't use steel rebar in our desert construction. Concrete is more durable that way," Hamida added as the pilot took them down.

Godfrey asked some questions about the costs and challenges of transporting building materials across the desert in a somewhat forced attempt at conversation. Their delegation's experts probably would have asked dozens of questions about the silica-salt skimmed here, but the only relevant question was whether the Arabs would consent to sell them any of it.

There weren't many people in the area outside the refinery. Oversized sliding doors made of dark wood dotted the perimeter, and a few workers stood near the parked machinery.

The pilot brought them down until the carpet hovered three feet off the sand. Hamida unfolded with typical Arabic flexibility, hopping off without waiting for assistance.

As Mike swung his legs over the side, the ambassador tapped him on the shoulder and whispered in his ear. "Your truth-telling magick is less important than the fact she sees you as Amy's brother. I know you don't like games, Mike, so you better start chewing on some of those lifesavers now."

This was why Mike hated diplomats. Godfrey just couldn't understand that there were limits to the amount of misdirections and omissions he could tolerate.

When he stepped off, Mike was immediately buffeted by a strong gust of hot air. The sand circled upward into clouds, though didn't appear to be forming into the more dangerous funnels. His new Arabian cloak blew tightly around his legs, and Mike had to untangle it before he could walk without fear of tripping.

Ambassador Godfrey stepped off the carpet and gasped, his forehead instantly beading with sweat. Hamida shot him a concerned look, then said something in Arabic to one of the were-jaguars, who hurried into the building.

"It's far too hot out here," Hamida said. "I sent Juan inside to get cooling caps for you both."

"I feel fine," Mike said, holding out his arms to let the cloak billow around him like a sail. "But the Danjou mages bought me this from the mall yesterday."

"That's one of the new aftermarket-enchanted bishts," Hamida said approvingly. "Not as good as a spell-woven one, but it'll do."

"I wish they'd brought me one," Godfrey griped. The ambassador had already unbuttoned his suit jacket and was now loosening his tie. "But I'll be alright in a minute. The heat just caught me by surprise."

Hamida made some joke about the carpet's air conditioning spells, while Mike walked past the building to get a better look at the fields. If Godfrey was going to start playing a diplomatic game, he'd rather put some distance between them.

The cloak's enchantment worked well; he only felt the heat against his cheeks. The brisk wind gave him the sensation of being blown in the face by a hair dryer. It wasn't uncomfortable per se, but did take some getting used to.

Now that they'd landed, the bleakness of the desert landscape took on a more artistic flair. From above, all Mike had seen was a pale, undulating blur. Here at ground level, the wind seemed to be carving shapes into the dunes, sculpting them like peaks of frosting to expose different layers of sand to the white-hot sun. It was still stark, but in an avant-garde, modern sense.

"Are you ready?"

Mike turned at the sound of Hamida's voice. The wind's rasp across the sand was so loud he hadn't heard her approach. Behind her, Juan handed Godfrey a shiny gold baseball cap that even a rap singer would consider gaudy. The embossed texture glinted in the sunlight, and Mike wondered if it were snakeskin.

Godfrey didn't hesitate to pull the cap on. Ordinarily, Mike was sure he'd have invented some diplomatic excuse to refuse, but he was clearly suffering. The ambassador's face was still flushed, and his dark suit now stained with sweat.

Two tails of gauzy gold fabric floated down the sides to drape over the ambassador's shoulders before being blown flat against his disheveled suit. Godfrey's expression of relief as the spell took effect was near-comical. Any attempt at dignity was lost as the gold fabric whipped around him, but at least he was now walking across the sand with more vigor.

"Here." Godfrey handed Mike a silver cap and began untangling the gold fabric that had wrapped around his torso.

Closer up, Mike could see the enchanted hats were

indeed made from some kind of reptile leather, with curtain-like pieces of shimmery silk fabric attached to the sides.

"Put it on," Godfrey insisted. "I don't want to be the only person wearing one of them."

Hamida's mouth quirked in a slight smile as Mike grudgingly took it. "Yes, put it on," she said. "I can't allow our honored guests to die of heat stroke."

Since he was already wearing the bisht, Mike didn't really need it to stay cool, but he couldn't let the ambassador be the only one to look like a fool.

"The enchantment is amazing!" Godfrey said, grabbing the fabric tails like a snake wrangler. "But what are these for?"

"We wrap the cloth around our faces like niqaabs to protect us from the wind-blown sand," Hamida said. "I'll help you adjust them before we tour the fields."

Mike could see the laughter in her eyes, and wondered if the were-jaguar had deliberately picked the most ridiculous-looking enchanted hats he could find.

The hot breeze rifled Mike's hair as he adjusted the backstrap. The moment Mike placed the hat on his head, the air quieted.

"Is it always this windy?" Godfrey asked, shading his eyes as he looked out.

Mike glanced at the silver fabric lying flat against his cloak, then out at the silica-salt field.

Hamida frowned. "Sometimes." *Truth.*

While the wind had stopped gusting around them, Mike could still see it rippling furrows in the sand dunes. Hamida must have also sensed something was off because she cocked her head to one side as she also took in the landscape.

"Why don't I show you the refinery first," she said, and gestured toward the whitewashed building.

Godfrey and Hamida began walking, but before Mike could follow, two tall, angular men with long sandy-blond hair and near-translucent faces stepped out of the air in front of him.

Mike took an abrupt step back. The other day, he'd been shocked when he looked outside the embassy to see a pair of wind faeries floating in the breeze. They'd disappeared as quickly as they'd appeared, and Mike had hoped he'd been mistaken.

These two shared the same lanky frames and pallor as the ones who had peeked through his embassy window. Unfortunately, they didn't seem ready to blow off anytime soon. One of them caught Mike's eyes, then turned to nod at his companion.

Mike took another small step back, holding his hands in front of him. *What are the vila doing here?* he wondered. Faeries drew power from greenery and growing things. For millennia, they had overlooked the Middle East in favor of the Taiga's rich woodlands and Asia's lush forests. No one — not even the overcautious junior staffers who'd written the briefing memos — thought there was any risk of a fae encounter in Arabia. And certainly not in the desert! Mike had miscalculated badly.

The man in pale green started to say something in a liquid, Slavic-sounding language, but Mike just shook his head as he inched away from them.

Hamida and Godfrey paused, turning back.

"Mike, aren't you coming?" Godfrey called. Neither he nor Hamida were reacting to the faeries' presence.

A funnel of sand swirled upward behind the vila. Mike took a bigger step back from the pair, whose eyes tracked his motions like cats waiting to pounce. The man in green tried again, this time in what sounded like Arabic.

Mike's heart pounded loudly enough that he could hear it thrumming against the sound of the blowing sand.

Hamida and Godfrey began walking back to Mike, angling their bodies against the wind. They were passed by two of the were-jaguars, who began bounding across the sand.

"Mister Michael, it's just a sudden sand spike. We get them from time to time," Hamida called out. "Let's go inside until the weather calms."

"Watch out!" Mike said, gesturing for the jaguars to stop. They clearly didn't see the faeries they were about to run into.

The were-jaguars' posture changed into a defensive position at his tone. Their yellow eyes glinted as they swung their heads around, examining the area.

The vila also saw his gesture and finally stopped speaking.

"Don't you see the wind fae?" Mike asked, pointing at the vila, who were now murmuring to each other in that incomprehensible language.

"Wind fae?" Hamida repeated in surprise, turning to where Mike had gestured. She pulled an iron rod from her pocket.

Her remaining bodyguards fanned out to scan the area, but none of them seemed to see what he did.

"I don't understand you," Mike said loudly to the vila.

The wind fae looked at each other.

"Where?" Godfrey asked in a low voice.

Mike pointed. "Right there. Two male vila, wearing pastel-colored tunics."

The jaguars sniffed the air, cautiously stepping around the

area Mike indicated. Abruptly, the wind died. The air became still so swiftly, Mike wondered if time had frozen. But the guards continued to circle the area, and stopping time was not reported to be among the fae's considerable magical powers.

The vila in pink pointed at Mike as he continued to talk to the other faerie. Mike wasn't sure whether it was better or worse that the pair were no longer trying to speak directly to him.

"Can you hear them?" Mike asked in desperation. No one could outrun a wind faerie.

Hamida gave him an assessing look. "I don't hear or see anything. We should go inside. These after-fabrication cooling spells on the bishts haven't been well-tested. Hallucinations are a common sign of heat stroke." *Truth.*

"I'm not hot," Mike said. He wished the Danjou mages were here to cast a revelation spell. Or better yet, one of Amy's werewolf guards. They had grown up on a fae preserve and would know what to do.

"Come on, Mike," Godfrey said patiently. "Let's get inside."

The vila in green nodded sharply, and the pair turned to look at Hamida.

The Amira inhaled. "I see them now," she said.

Hamida used her rod to push Mike behind her, then let it dangle from one hand as she spread her arms wide in either an invitation or provocation. Mike wasn't sure which.

It must have meant something to the vila though, because the sand swirled around them, hiding them within the eye of a cyclone and separating them from the wereguards. The rasp of sand should have been deafening, but Mike felt like he was wearing noise-canceling headphones.

"I don't see anything!" Godfrey said as he spun around, his voice loud in the heavy silence. A grain of sand escaped the whirlwind, ricocheting in a swirl of gray and green. It struck the ambassador directly in the eye.

The vila in pink began speaking to Hamida in Arabic.

Truth. The clear flavor of their exchange didn't taste as refreshing as it usually did. Mike's mouth was too sour with the taste of fear.

Godfrey stepped back, and Mike assumed he could see the vila now. He wished the ambassador would translate, but it was probably best if they both stayed quiet. Hamida had taken ownership of this confrontation, and it was hard to say what might offend the fae.

Why are they here? Mike worried. Faeries avoided deserts almost as much as they avoided iron-rich cities. Yet they had appeared outside the embassy. Mike was deeply afraid that *he* was the reason for their unusual presence.

Hamida's back-and-forth with the two vila continued for a tense minute before the Amira bowed her head.

"English?" the vila in green asked in that language.

"English," Hamida replied with a curt nod.

The wind gusted again, dissolving the sand cyclone in an outward spray that blasted the stalking jaguars. The weres shook off the deluge and bounded after the vila. But as suddenly as they'd come, the pair disappeared. All of them searched the silica-salt field for any sign of the faeries.

The stirring of sand and the ripples up the dunes caught Mike's eye. He pointed at what first looked like a waver of heated air above the sand. He blinked, and saw two men climbing the air like they were ascending a staircase. Then the breeze blew them away.

One of the were-jaguars snapped at the empty air, disappearing down the other side of the dune as another continued to prowl the perimeter.

Mike turned when Hamida cursed.

"Are they gone?" she asked him. The faint lines around her eyes had deepened.

"I don't know. Maybe," he replied.

"The vila hunt like djinni, always listening, always circling," one of the were-jaguars said in her Spanish-accented English.

"What did they say?" Mike asked.

"They wanted to know why you wouldn't answer them," Godfrey said when Hamida didn't answer. "She told them you didn't speak Arabic and probably not Uralic, either." *Truth.*

Mike shook his head. "I only speak English. Where did they go? Did they say whether they were coming back?"

"I'm curious why they're here in the first place," Godfrey murmured, giving Mike a hard look.

"They said they've gone to learn English so they can welcome you properly to Arabia," Hamida answered.

The taste of Hamida's omission made Mike swallow hard.

"What are you leaving out?" he asked sharply.

"That is what I discussed with the fae," Hamida answered just as sharply.

"They wanted the Amira to introduce them to you, but she said that wasn't her place. That her brother had charge of the American delegation," Godfrey explained.

"Which is the truth, though a bit fussy," Hamida said.

The were-jaguar nodded approvingly. "Buy time so we can regroup. Good plan."

"I am just surprised at their presence." Hamida looked out at the jaguars prowling across the dunes. "Before today, I *never* spoke to a vila. Never even saw one before. Khalid is the only Arab alive known to encounter them. The East Wind's vila get bored and like to play with his djinni."

"I can't cast spells at all," Mike assured her. "And Amir Khalid is the only mage who can conjure a djinn."

"They have to know that." Hamida flicked her gaze over him before refocusing on the dunes. "But they want something from you." *Truth.*

Mike swallowed hard. Hamida was quite likely correct.

"Call Vizier Malik on our way back to the city," the jaguar suggested. "He has helped Al-Amir negotiate with the fae before."

Hamida nodded, but her focus was on the place where the vila had vanished.

"Michael Arnold is your honored guest," Godfrey stated firmly. *Truth.*

Legal or not, Mike was pretty sure the ambassador would sell his own mother to the fae if it meant securing a silica-salt deal. It was surprising that Godfrey would make such a point, but the ambassador did succeed in redirecting Hamida's attention. She gave Mike a firm nod.

"We guard our honored guests as our own," Hamida declared.

Mike was relieved to taste her absolute truth.

"Amira, we must return," the jaguar said. "*Now.*"

Her reverie broken, Amira Hamida began calling out orders to the pilots. Within moments, their group had reboarded the carpets. As they flew back, Mike stared at the undulating dunes and wondered what kind of welcome the fae were planning.

3

RIYADH, ARABIA

KHALID LOOKED up from his tablet, squinting as he assessed the line of late afternoon sun slanting across the casting field's sand. *Only a few hours till sunset,* he thought. If Loujain's son were to have any chance of casting the spell, Malik needed to get him here before then.

A dozen sub-viziers and their aides sat crammed together on the stone benches by the wall. His nephew Farouk didn't enjoy casting before an audience, but they would need witnesses if they were going to position this properly for the press.

Khalid looked down at his tablet. It was easier to concentrate now that there was a crisis. *The doctor has not completely hijacked my attention,* Khalid thought as he adjusted the rockers in the second layer of the spell schematic.

The door in the wall opened, and Malik walked through, followed by Khalid's nephew.

"I need a few more minutes to make the adjustments, then we can get started," Khalid called, then beckoned his nephew closer. "Farouk, come here. I want to show you what I'm doing."

Everyone stood, offering Malik their seats, but the Prime Minister waived them off and began speaking quietly with the Vizier of Media Relations. Farouk kicked off his loafers, placing them neatly by the wall, before walking across the silica-salt encrusted sand to join Khalid in the center of the field.

His nephew was dressed to go out, wearing the kind of tight-cut clubbing style the youth favored. It was early for such pastimes, and Khalid supposed that was how Malik managed to collect the boy so quickly.

Khalid tapped the tablet, recalibrating the backward flow to increase the number of djinn that would be conjured.

He didn't often cast a swarming spell — not even during their regular defense exercises. For too many Arabs, the sight of a djinn swarm conjured traumatic memories of the uprising more than a decade past.

Besides, it was high time Farouk proved his mettle, and the pundits would likely interpret the timing of this "test" as a thinly-veiled warning to their American guests.

"Vizier Malik didn't explain why you wanted to see me," Farouk said in his light tenor. "What are you casting?"

Khalid held up one finger while making the final modifications with the electronic pen. Farouk's primary schema for perceiving magick was one of Khalid's secondaries, so it wasn't difficult to edit the design in his nephew's preferred language.

He tapped save, then handed Farouk his tablet. "Take a look."

Loujain's third son had proven more competent with silica-salt enchanting than his older brothers. So when the whispers about Loujain's failing health and Khalid's lack of mage offspring erupted into a rather unpleasant tabloid crisis, Farouk had been the obvious choice.

The Quatrone had acknowledged him as Heir to the House of Khalid two years ago. Which had been quite a relief to Farouk's brothers, who imagined they'd escaped the demands of learning the complex djinn enchantments.

Their respite would be short-lived. Once Farouk mastered the spells, Khalid planned to train Loujain's other sons: all of them drew enough power and had the requisite precision in their perception to conjure a djinn. They just needed to increase their stamina. Arabia was too dependent on Khalid right now, and he didn't want that burden to pass to his successor.

Farouk flipped back between the second and third stages of the spell. "Why the modifications?"

"We only need to use the location aspect of the swarming djinn spell. There's no need to arm them."

"Why the swarming variation at all? Won't that be overkill?" Farouk looked troubled.

"We're chasing faeries. They can evade a single djinn, but not a thousand-and-one," Khalid replied, trying to focus on today's problem and not the problems of the past. "The American truth-teller is our honored guest. The fact that the vila have singled him out is too unusual to ignore."

Farouk's brow furrowed as he examined the spell.

While daylight was fading, Khalid didn't rush him. His nephew drew sufficient power, and Khalid thought he had the stamina. Farouk had failed last time only because nothing was really at stake. A real crisis couldn't be manufactured, and only in the crucible of a crisis could a person truly discover their full potential.

Vizier Malik walked over. "Until now, the only faerie sightings in the last eighty-three years have centered on Al-

Amir." He clapped Khalid's shoulder. "He is the mage who developed the djinn spell."

"This unusual interest in our American guest is concerning," Khalid added quietly.

Farouk nodded, still flicking through the pages of the spell. The swarming djinn element was one of the more complex variants.

"Do you think the Americans made a bargain with the vila?" Farouk asked, looking up.

Khalid shook his head. "No. The vila answer to the East Wind, and she has sworn never to bargain with my enemies."

"Truth-tellers are faerie changelings. Perhaps they see a kinship with him," Farouk suggested.

"That would be the best outcome," Malik agreed. "But the fae are unpredictable. The American werewolf insists on coming with us to investigate. While I would ordinarily refuse, their delegation is also alarmed."

"And he is Doctor Amy's vizier, not part of the American government's security detail," Farouk said, a slight wrinkle forming between his eyes. "They don't know about your bargain with the East Wind, do they, Uncle?"

Khalid and Malik exchanged a look. Malik wasn't fond of Farouk, but even he would have to acknowledge the boy's political acumen.

"Only the Saaqib leadership is aware of Al-Amir's bargain with the East Wind," Malik said stiffly.

Khalid suppressed a sigh. His prime minister refused to see that Farouk was almost as clever as Faiza in these matters.

"Your bargain aside, healing my mother is a safer pathway to reopening the silica-salt trade than asking the fae for help," Farouk pointed out. "We need to be prepared for what the Americans might do if their doctor fails."

"They need our silica-salt so desperately, there's nothing they won't do," Khalid said. *But I'm clean,* he thought. *They haven't cast anything on me yet.*

Malik and Farouk continued to speculate on the possibility of an American plot. Khalid looked on, relieved that his vizier wasn't dismissing his nephew outright. Malik might never be Farouk's friend, but at least he was treating the boy with respect. After a while, Khalid pointed to Farouk's tablet.

"Cast that spell, Nephew, and no one will doubt you've earned your place in the succession."

Malik nodded. Even he couldn't argue with that. Farouk swallowed hard, focusing intently on the schematic.

"It's not easy to find vila who don't want to be found, so ensuring a large volume of djinni in the area is necessary." Khalid tapped the screen to enlarge a portion of the spell schematic. "See the adjustments here."

Khalid gave his nephew a moment to study before zooming out. "The swarm is cast in four stages." He flicked the screen of the tablet through each diagram. "The final stage is the hardest because you have to maintain the outline of magick in the first three while you cast the final components."

Farouk nodded. "You want me to cast the last stage."

"I want you to cast all of them."

His nephew's eyes widened. This was a bit of a gamble. Farouk hadn't even managed a basic djinn spell on his own yet. All djinn spells required the caster to maintain sustained concentration, but the swarm variation was the most challenging in this regard.

"Are you sure, Uncle?" Farouk asked quietly, staring at the schematic for the final stage.

"I need you," Khalid replied. Which wasn't *quite* true, at least not at this precise moment, but it was true enough.

"Once the djinni locate the vila, I need to negotiate with them. If I'm too drained from casting this spell, I'm apt to make a mistake."

Farouk swallowed. "I can do it."

If Farouk failed, Khalid would cast it and let Malik take the lead bargaining with the fae. But Khalid really hoped his nephew succeeded. It would make for an ideal news report, and Amy's werewolf would surely tell her how smoothly Khalid handled the delicate negotiation.

"Whenever you're ready," Khalid said, gesturing toward the center of the field.

Farouk hesitated. "I'd like to follow this." He held up the tablet.

"Of course," Khalid said. "Let duelers cast their simplistic spells from memory. There's no shame in following a guide."

Farouk looked encouraged by that and strode into the middle of the field. There were larger casting fields on the palace grounds, but this walled-in enclosure boasted a double-depth of silica-salt encrusted sand. This field didn't merely absorb magical backlash. It provided a steady source of ambient magick to fuel a complex casting. And since the sun was swiftly fading, Farouk might well need the boost.

His nephew started out well: the gold hashwork provided a good base for the next stage, and Farouk took his time pulling the lines taut before moving on to the aqua-tinged checkerboard pattern.

Layering was key to the djinn spell. Most enchantments only used a single stage, or at most, serial castings where the mage could rest between workings. But to craft a djinn from pure magick and air without providing it commands would be reckless: there was no telling what kind of uncontrolled and mindless destruction might follow.

So instead, Khalid had discovered how to enchant the djinn in stages. It was an exercise in power, precision, and, critically, endurance.

Farouk stood in the classic mage stance: feet widespread, shoulders back. Even holding the tablet, he looked like a great mage. Khalid typically sat on the sand to cast a djinn swarm, but given the audience he'd assembled, his nephew's pose was for the best.

Farouk didn't hesitate as he pushed his power outward to cast the first stages. His steady lines shone orange and blue atop a glimmering net of gold circles, but by the time he began stage three, the network of red and teal loops had started vibrating.

"That's all right," Khalid said, moving beside him. "Well within tolerance. The trick is to reduce the inward twist in this next stage." Khalid pointed to the diagram on Farouk's tablet, tracing the flow.

"By how much, do you think?" Beads of sweat dotted Farouk's brow.

"Just a hair. Not much. You don't want to reduce the number of djinni that will emerge. Keep going. You're doing great."

Farouk started the final stage, his arms shaking with the effort. He was casting more slowly than Khalid did — which made it significantly harder to complete the enchantment, but then he didn't have Khalid's experience and probably didn't want to risk making a mistake.

"Tie it off now," Khalid ordered sharply. Farouk's face had lost its sparkle, but the sheen of sweat had disguised his magical exhaustion in the fading light.

Farouk pushed his power one last time, activating the final stage and pulling taut the lines of magick that he'd layered into the spell. As his nephew crumpled onto the sand, a thousand-and-one swirls of magick condensed out of the air.

How handsome my heir is, Khalid thought, staring at the swarm of Farouk-topped djinni before kneeling down beside his nephew and pressing his fingers on his wrist. The sluggish beat told him Farouk was more alive than the thousand-and-one Farouk-styled simulacrums overhead.

For three centuries, he'd watched oversized images of himself destroying everything and everyone in their path. Tonight, for the first time since that one fate-changing day in Delphi, the djinni overhead wore someone else's face.

Khalid looped a line of his personal power around the horde. "Find the vila who spoke with Hamida bint Hisham al-Saaqib today."

The spell flared purple and silver as Khalid's command gave the djinni purpose. The swarm swirled upward into the twilight so fast, the sound of the collapsing vacuum left in their wake clapped like thunder.

The sonoluminescence of the djinni's flight across the desert would be visible to mundanes and mages alike, and many would be wondering — no, *fearing* — what the release of a thousand-and-one djinni meant.

Within the hour, the palace press advisor would release an article regarding Farouk's accomplishment. Too many people remembered the hunts a decade past. With the Americans here, it would be better for people to see this as a training exercise: a demonstration of power intended to warn their visitors that even without Khalid to guard their borders, Arabia would not bow to a suzerain.

4

ABU DHABI, ARABIA

KHALID HAD NEVER SPOKEN to the East Wind's vila directly. The handful of times they had appeared, Eurus herself had always led the conversation. But her two companions had seemed to enjoy sporting with his djinni. Tonight's hunt might seem like a game to them — or at least an invitation to play.

He couldn't imagine that the two vila who had surprised Hamida today were anyone other than Eurus's attendants. Arabia's deserts might be prized by mages for their silica-salt, but apart from the East Wind, the fae had no interest in its barren sands. Unfortunately, knowing who they probably were didn't give Khalid any better insight into what they wanted.

Satellite imagery revealed the djinni were headed toward the eastern coast. While Doppler radar couldn't identify the constructs directly, it did track the lightning that trailed beneath the miniature whirlwind constructs.

Since the swarm could travel the desert at the speed of sound, there was no point in attempting to follow their trails via carpet. Instead, Khalid, Malik, and Nimchuk,

Amy's werewolf vizier, boarded an Arabian military jet toward Abu Dhabi, where the thousand-and-one djinni had converged.

By the time the plane landed, glowing red and gold djinni trails crossed the night sky like a loosely-woven veil. The djinni had already been combing the area for hours. It *was* almost like a game — though on the few occasions the fae had approached Khalid for such sport, they had agreed on the rules of the hunt in advance.

"The vila have already left the city," Malik said in passable English as the three men boarded the small carpet. "The djinni are converging in the desert." He gestured north, and the pilot nodded.

The pilot may not have understood the English Malik was speaking for Nimchuk's benefit, but she understood the directive and steered the carpet northward at top speed.

"They're herding the vila," Khalid said, pointing at the bright flashes in the sky. "See the flares?"

"But where?" Nimchuk rumbled. "Are there any oases nearby? Even the wind fae prefer trees to sand."

Malik frowned. "You're probably right — but the Liwa Oasis is over a hundred kilometers away."

The red-gold djinni trails grew brighter as they passed over the city line, a sign that the constructs had traced and retraced the same path. Khalid felt his pulse pound. He wasn't a battlemage like his younger sister, but he was battle-tested. And unlike an actual battle, there was a thrill to this kind of hunt.

"The vila may be doubling back," Khalid said. "There's a large mangrove park in the city. The djinni are faster than they are. If I were them, I'd head toward the closest power center."

Nimchuk nodded. "As long as you didn't stake the park with iron and steel, that seems right."

"We never had the need. Arabia isn't overrun with fae like America," Malik said. "Let's go."

The pilot turned back. By now, the djinni were swarming directly overhead, lighting the air around them with sparkling funnels of energy that illuminated the dark city. The governor must have ordered a blackout to avoid attracting the attention of both the hunters and the hunted. While this swarm wasn't coded to kill, it was usually suicide to come between the djinni and their prey.

Jubail Mangrove Park was a nature sanctuary filled with a half-submerged forest of mangrove trees. Trails of wooden walkways snaked through the Persian Gulf's brackish water, allowing pedestrians to experience the lush greenery without getting wet.

The pilot ignored the no-flying signs, wending their carpet mere inches above the walkways at a breakneck pace. Overhead, the djinni's convergence was growing ever brighter until the reddish glow of the djinni overtook the moon, and the water's surface gleamed pink.

Even if he couldn't see the wind fae themselves, he could feel the thrumming whirlwind as Farouk's djinni surrounded the vila.

"There," Khalid pointed left.

Despite the violence in the cyclone-driven air, he felt remarkably calm. Now was the time for bargaining, not spell-slinging. He would discover what these faeries wanted from Amy's brother and prove to her his ability to protect his own. Khalid stood, fighting to remain upright against the wind that was overpowering the carpet's shielding spell.

When he finally positioned himself, he called out in Arabic.

"Have I got your attention, vila?"

A shaft of lightning blasted out from beneath a djinn,

cleaving a mangrove in half. The smell of burnt wood and ozone competed with the swamp's sulfuric odor. The pilot cautiously steered them closer to the djinni's points of light.

The carpet's shielding spells were well-constructed, but they would not withstand a direct blast. So Malik held a no-pass shield spell at the ready, the black-rimmed hashwork near-complete as they headed under the low-flying, Farouk-topped army. As they drew closer to the dense center where the djinni had herded the faeries, the rush of wind grew louder.

The pilot approached cautiously until they reached the epicenter of the swarm. Above them, the sky was completely hidden by djinni cyclones spinning into each other. A chaotic ceiling of red lightning zagging in all directions blurred the individual outlines of each spinning djinn. The vila were here. Somewhere.

"Did you enjoy the game?" Khalid called out.

"You don't think of this as a game, so that spoils the fun," came the sullen response, just audible over the sound of the djinni.

The pilot didn't need to be prompted to head in that direction. She flew cautiously, opting to wend around the mangrove trees instead of risking close contact with the gusting cyclones.

Khalid hoped the pair turned out to be Dayan and Dimitri. If not, this would mean more faeries had blown into his desert.

The pilot banked a hard right between two trees, and they emerged in a clearing surrounded by densely-growing mangroves, whose canopy almost covered the sky. The djinni's cyclone tails twisted overhead, sending a swirling plume of pure magick to coat the leaves. It reminded Khalid of the frost-coated grass he'd seen on his visit to the Mongolian plains.

"Will you meet with us?" Khalid asked, searching the area for a sign of a faerie hiding in the wind.

"Since you've made such an effort to track us down, I suppose we can spare a moment."

Before Khalid could speak, Nimchuk tapped him on the shoulder and pointed. Khalid looked down.

"Take care. We've stumbled into a faerie circle," Amy's vizier warned.

While Khalid could still feel the djinni thrumming in his bones, the sound of their cyclones was more muted than their proximity would ordinarily suggest. He looked around more closely, noticing a slight shimmer in the reddish air around them. The werewolf was right.

The djinni still hovered overhead but were held back from the clearing. While the suffocating haze of djinn trails made it difficult to see the circle clearly, Khalid had a hunch their carpet was trapped within its perimeter. The fae sense of fairness required any faerie caught by a human to grant them a boon. But while their djinni might have hounded the vila into this clearing, the faeries had managed to turn the tables. The hunted had become the hunters.

Khalid wasn't entirely sure how to regain the advantage. He held his palms upright in the universal gesture of peace and glanced around, looking for some sign of the hidden fae. "It would be easier to converse if you'd show yourselves," he said.

A hazy white face emerged on the left. Khalid blinked as the empty air gradually filled with the figure of an angular man wearing a pink tunic. He hovered cross-legged beside another male faerie wearing pale green. Both had long blond hair that floated behind them in the breeze.

"That's better," Khalid said, inclining his head solemnly to each vila, who responded to his greeting in kind. They looked like Dayan and Dimitri, but he wasn't sure who was who. When Eurus had introduced them, her presence had been too overwhelming for Khalid to take close note of her entourage.

"Were you able to learn English? My companion doesn't speak Arabic." Khalid gestured to Nimchuk.

The first vila's face turned toward the werewolf. "You've come with the Americans," he said in English.

"Yes," Nimchuk rumbled in his deep voice.

They glanced at each other, then back at the were. Both wore an avid expression of interest. The fae were so unpredictable. You could never tell what would catch their attention. And Khalid knew how unrelenting in their obsessions the wind fae could be.

"Vizier Nimchuk leads the were honor guard protecting Doctor Amy Bant," Khalid said.

The vila's pale eyes flickered from Nimchuk back to Khalid, dismissing the packleader.

At least they aren't obsessed with Amy, Khalid thought, and a part of him recognized how absurd his sense of relief was.

Nimchuk stood up. He was a foot taller than Khalid and powerfully built. Weres were not immune to fae magick, but the wolf had an intimidating presence all the same. "Doctor Bant is the truth-teller's sister-in-law," Nimchuk announced. "His name is Michael Arnold, and he is Amir Khalid's honored guest."

The faeries' eyes lit up.

Khalid knew he had to be careful. The vila couldn't hear everything spoken in the air like the elementals who birthed them. While Eurus never fully understood the value of information, often under- or over-estimating its importance, the vila might not be as ignorant.

"Why are you so interested in the American changeling?" Khalid asked, feigning only mild curiosity.

The faerie dressed in green raised one eyebrow quizzi-
cally. "Why should we tell you?"

Although they didn't fall for his ploy, Khalid recognized
the invitation to bargain. But before he could respond,
Nimchuk sprung.

The were became a blurred glitter of magick, changing
from man to wolf even as he leapt. It was an insane move:
the vila's magical ability to stop the air from moving made
them invulnerable. At least that's what Khalid used to
think.

The gray wolf hit the vila in the green tunic, tumbling
him off his perch and splashing into the brackish water
below. The shimmering colors indicative of fae magick
swirled around them, and the scent of growing things, dark
and rich, erupted. Either the werewolf or the vila had trig-
gered an enchantment. The smell was so strong, Khalid
could taste it.

The vila in pink turned, his face fixed in shock. So it
must have been Nimchuk who had somehow altered the
faerie circle's protective magick.

Streaks of red and gold whistled past as the djinni began
pouring into the clearing. Their supersonic vibrations made
Khalid's jaw reverberate. He ignored the sensation as he
focused his mage-sight on the faerie circle spell hidden
beneath the blur of the flying constructs. The djinni had
been constructed to seek, not destroy. Now that their
mission was completed, their presence was more
distracting than dangerous. No, the real danger lay with the
vila who had conjured the circle.

Malik must have reached the same conclusion. His
vizier jumped up, reaching into his pocket for his steel fan.
Khalid took Malik's arm before he could pull it out.

"Wait," Khalid mouthed, pointing his chin at the vila in
pale pink.

The faerie fluttered onto his back, his arms and legs stretching outward as if he were swimming in the air. His long hair drifted like a halo around him, and he reached one hand up, his wrist bent in a languid gesture.

"Ahh, wolf! That is a rich spell!" The vila kicked and floated higher, ignoring the djinni thrumming around him. Somehow, the wind faerie was able to make his voice heard over the near-incapacitating noise of the djinn swarm.

Khalid looked down. The water was shallow, but Nimchuk and the other vila were completely submerged. The fae magick continued to bubble outward from the pair, enveloping the mangroves and twining around the faerie circle in lines of gold and variegated greens. The plaid pattern pulled taut. The crystalline music of a brass bell rang out. Its heavy reverberations echoed around the clearing, rippling the water with streaks of sound.

A geyser fountained upward, blowing Nimchuk and the green-clad vila up. The dripping faerie's eyes were closed in a blissful expression as he arched his back and floated atop the air, his arms crossed in a cradle for his head.

The smell of wet fur overpowered the woodsy scent as Nimchuk landed gracefully back on the carpet. The sheen of the were-spell flickered, and the wolf changed back to man. Malik handed Nimchuk his abandoned robe.

"That was more refreshment than I've had in a decade," sighed the vila in pink. "What was that?"

"Woodwife magick," the other vila called and sat upright. "I haven't tasted the northern forests in so long."

He sounded rather wistful.

Khalid hoped Nimchuk knew what he was doing. Woodwives could kill you with their kindness.

Gusts of hot air blew around the vila in pink like an oversized hair dryer. "How long will the spell last?"

Nimchuk shrugged.

Despite the incessant thrum of the djinni, the forest felt calmer somehow. Mangrove trees were not tall, but those anchored by the taut lines had become fatter, greener. A different kind of tree with thick gray bark and notched leaves now emerged in the center of the circle, spearing high into the sky so that the djinni had to swirl around it. Lightning strikes from their cyclones bounced off its bark, spattering harmlessly into the air and careening down in a shower of gold sparks.

Khalid squinted at the entwined faerie spells. Fae magick worked differently than mage magick, but their roots were similar. He was only now beginning to discern the original purpose of the vila's circle spell. Nimchuk's fast action may have saved them all.

"However did you earn a fae blessing?" asked the vila in pink. "This feels like a year-and-a-day boon."

"It's coopted your circle," Khalid said flatly, but they didn't react. Perhaps they were so seduced by the preserve that they didn't mind losing their greatest weapon. Or perhaps they just couldn't hear him. The noise of all thousand-and-one djinni was deafening. The constructs were swarming so closely, he could feel their resonance in his ribs. They couldn't negotiate with the djinni spinning around.

I don't need to arm them, Khalid told himself firmly, though he didn't find it easy to give up his own weapons.

Khalid pushed his power out along the lead that connected him to the spell. Like most acts of undoing, disenchanting the djinn spell was much easier than casting it in the first place. Within moments, the air cleared, and the light of the quarter moon filtered through the mangroves to glisten on the now-quiet water below.

His ears rang with the sudden absence of sound.

"Much better," sighed one of the vila dreamily. "Without

your creatures buzzing, I can think clearly. Amir Khalid, introduce us to your new were."

Khalid shook his head. "Not my were. He is Doctor Amy's vizier. Followers of Eurus, be known to Packleader Nimchuk of the Blue Hills Preserve."

"I'm Dayan, and this is Dimitri," the vila in green said to Nimchuk. "Your spell is marvelous! I can feel the forest of she whose power fueled it."

"You remember my Prime Vizier, Malik?" Khalid gestured toward him.

The two fae nodded, and Malik responded in kind. Formality was the safest approach with the fae.

Khalid didn't introduce the pilot so the pair would understand she wouldn't be participating in their games. He would have left his were-guard out as well, but the American wolf had decided to get more actively involved than Khalid expected.

Nimchuk had taken quite a risk by attacking the vila. Ordinarily, a wind faerie could stop the air in an instant, but Khalid could see the lines of stress on the vila's faces.

"The djinni were not sent to harm you," Malik assured them.

"I'd forgotten how utterly exhausting it is to outrun your djinni," Dimitri said, shaking his wet hair. A shower of pinkish magick rained down.

Khalid wondered how close the faeries had been to fading when they'd enchanted their faerie circle. He was afraid he had miscalculated badly in sending the swarm.

"This taste of pine trees and moss is most refreshing," Dayan said, his pale eyes fluttering shut. He let his head roll back in evident delight. "Where is the woodwife who gave you this spell?"

"In the United States. Massachusetts." Nimchuk replied.

The wolf's face and expression gave nothing away. He was the consummate soldier.

"Mass-a-chu-setts," Dimitri savored the word. "I wish I were there."

Dayan fondled the mangrove's leaves. "It even feels like a pine."

The two spoke to one another in Uralic while petting the trees.

"That fae circle they built—" Khalid began in a low voice.

"Their circle was a suicide bomb," Nimchuk interrupted softly. "I've never seen faeries so depleted."

Khalid nodded grimly. He'd finally discerned the original enchantment's framework. The circle had been primed to implode with at least a mach eight velocity.

"I'm not sure how long these two have been flitting about in your deserts, but they need to go home," Nimchuk continued in a firm tone.

Khalid couldn't agree more. The vila followed the East Wind and seemed to enjoy "playing" with the djinni as much as she did, but perhaps tonight's misadventure would convince them to return to the Taiga.

"So these fae are desperate unto fading," Malik mused. "That might give us the advantage."

"We need to know what they want with Michael Arnold," Khalid said. "Then we can determine how to deal with them."

"I grew up in a faerie forest trading favors with the fae. Will you let me bargain with them on your behalf?" Nimchuk asked.

Khalid hesitated. The werewolf certainly had greater insight than he did. Nimchuk had noticed the vila's condition and acted swiftly to assert the advantage.

Malik's lips tightened in warning. His advisor was right

to be cautious: the wolf was an American. Nevertheless, common threats could build firm alliances.

"You have the greater experience," Khalid said slowly. The wolf's expression was unreadable, but Khalid decided to take a leap of faith. "Can you find out what they want with the truth-teller?"

Nimchuk nodded, then turned to the fae who were twining themselves about the trunks of the trees as if they were dryads and not vila.

"Dimitri," Nimchuk called. He had to repeat himself a few times before the faerie looked at him. "Why have you stayed so long in this barren desert?"

"A gift such as you've given us certainly warrants an answer to that."

Nimchuk raised his eyes. "And then some. The game is mine to choose."

"We are honest in our bargains." Dayan sounded insulted.

Nimchuk didn't rise to the bait. "You are vila. Honor-keepers. I'd expect nothing less."

"But you're also reputed to be plain-spoken," Malik added. "So far, you haven't lived up to that part of the vila's reputation."

Nimchuk glared at the Prime Minister.

Dimitri laughed. "So that is to be the game, then. A game of plain-spokenness. We accept."

Khalid wasn't certain what had just happened but decided it would be best to let the wolf speak for them at this point. "Enough, Malik. Let Nimchuk deal with the fae."

A green glow swirled through the air of the clearing, something citrusy in flavor but bright in texture. It was questing almost, wrapping him in scent and taste.

"You owe me the courtesy of a full response before you tease our truths from us," Nimchuk rumbled.

"My games are like Romani dances. I always build to a crescendo." Dimitri's answer didn't make any sense to Khalid, but he had the sinking suspicion he'd soon understand the faerie's meaning all too well.

"We were playing in the Saharan currents with Eurus when she encountered a djinn and became intrigued," Dayan said. "While we returned to the Taiga, she stayed behind, fascinated by your magick."

Dimitri traced a line that flared blue, and Khalid felt as if he had just sipped lemonade.

They're making me taste their truth, as if I were a changeling like Amy's brother, Khalid realized.

"Num, who rules the Taiga, wasn't happy that we'd 'abandoned' one of the last elementals," Dayan said. "After Lord Ares killed Zephyr in that foolish game, he grew concerned and sent us back to keep Eurus company."

"Zephyr's dead?" Khalid was shocked. He hadn't expected the elemental faerie to return after being confined to physical form, but he'd never expected this. Even reduced in power, Zephyr was still formidable. "When did this happen?"

Nimchuk raised an eyebrow. "Forty, maybe fifty years ago. How well did you know the South Wind?"

"I met him once." Khalid's mouth watered as Dimitri's spell teased his palate with the flavor of unripened dates. It was so hard not to explain, to hold back from telling them about that horrible day in Delphi's caves. He swallowed hard and clenched his jaw tight.

Nimchuk waited, but it was Dayan who broke the silence.

"A momentous meeting," the vila said. "Shall I tell you about it, wolf? It was back in 1907—"

"Lord Num owes Eurus a debt," Nimchuk interrupted.

Eurus had never mentioned her brother after they left

Delphi, and Khalid had never asked. He worried she might hold him responsible for Zephyr's lost power. With the fae, it was better to say less than more. But now Dimitri's spell invited Khalid's confession, tantalizing his mouth with the sharp promise of new grapes.

"Give to get, wolf," Dimitri prompted. "This pair did not know of Zephyr's demise. A game of truths requires each player to take their turn."

Dayan's blue eyes bored into Khalid's. "Who is the American changeling to you? Can you bargain for him?"

Khalid swallowed hard. Both faeries were starting to look better. Their moonlit faces were still pale but not as pasty-white as they'd been.

His stomach churned under the force of Dimitri's spell. He wanted to say the changeling was an obligation and nothing more, but the words formed within his thoughts, aching to break free:

I love him because I love her.

"Michael Arnold is my honored guest," Khalid said sharply, as much to himself as to the vila who watched him so closely. "I'm duty-bound to ensure his safety while he remains within Arabian borders."

He hesitated, and the slightly floral scent of Amy's skin mixed with the acerbic scent of her soap confused him, teased him. The truth-teller was Amy's brother. Siblings were as one person under the law. Khalid clenched his jaw, but the words erupted from his lips unbidden.

"Even after he leaves, he'll remain under my protection!"

Khalid clamped his mouth closed. He hadn't intended to share more than the American's status as his guest. But they were as one. He couldn't, wouldn't, allow any faerie to hurt Amy. Use her as they used him. Toy with her. Scare her—

The taste of lemonade filled his mouth, enticing him to elaborate.

Khalid blinked to clear his vision. He couldn't stop talking now that he'd begun. In desperation, he pushed his power outward to build a shield, but the taste lingered, the acidic citric sweetness burning a hole in his middle.

"Give to get, Dayan," Nimchuk said in his deep voice, and the vila's spell loosened around Khalid as it fixed on the faerie.

"We stay in the desert because we were commanded to do so," Dayan said.

The flavor of ripe strawberries competed with the lingering floral scent Khalid couldn't quite shake.

"Lord Num worries that Eurus will dissolve into air, fade into oblivion before his debt can be expiated," Dimitri added. "But I no longer care if she does. I just want to go home!"

Failing to satisfy a debt was a kind of moral wound for the fae. They were haunted by their outstanding debts much as Khalid was haunted by his wartime errors. While he didn't wish that kind of suffering on anyone, he wouldn't allow Num to use Amy to spare himself pain.

"We have less to complain about than the vila who were trapped in iron-strewn Yorkshire with Titania..." Dayan's voice tapered off.

The taste of blood oranges burst upon Khalid's tongue, and Dayan's face twisted.

"Yet now Titania's fae have escaped to the Congo, and we are still enduring the lifeless desert!" Dayan spat the last word.

Then go back to where you came from! It took every ounce of self-control Khalid could muster to keep that thought contained. This was his land, and the fae only caused problems.

"What do you want with the changeling?" Nimchuk asked Dimitri in a voice that was more growl than question.

Khalid was once again glad for the wolf's forceful intervention. Khalid had already revealed too much, and Amy was again invading his thoughts. She was like a spell in his blood. He needed to forget her, but he longed to see her again.

"Can *you* bargain for Michael Arnold, wolf?" Dimitri asked.

"Within limits," Nimchuk answered. "He has given me some authority."

Dimitri nodded at Dayan.

Khalid bit his tongue hard enough that the coppery taste of blood washed away the crispness of Nimchuk's truth. What was the wolf to Amy? Could he bargain on her behalf as well? The idea burned a dark hole in his belly.

Dayan blew a bubble of dull green air that shimmered as it enveloped the clearing. Khalid's ears popped. He could no longer hear the sound of wind in the trees or the light lapping of water. The vila had cast a silencing spell, surrounding them in a livable vacuum.

Khalid tensed. Dayan was trying to conceal them from the East Wind. *The fae are immortal but not unkillable,* he reminded himself, regretting his decision to dissolve the swarm instead of arming it. Bringing Nimchuk was foolish. If the vila acted, both he and the wolf might fall, depriving Amy of her best protection.

"Your American changeling looks exactly like Zephyr," Dimitri said, his voice oddly flat as the magick absorbed its sound.

"Exactly," Dayan emphasized.

Khalid frowned. If Zephyr had dallied with a human woman, was it possible that his ever-present sister didn't know about it? Was this a ruse?

"Do you believe Michael Arnold is Zephyr's son?" Nimchuk asked.

The question echoed like a struck gong, and the entire clearing seemed to hold its breath for the answer.

"He is the right age and appearance," Dimitri said in a failed attempt to seem indifferent.

"Eurus must judge for herself," Dayan added piously.

Khalid narrowed his eyes. "What are the rules of your game, Dimitri? Malik challenged you to a game of truths, yet you dabble in subterfuge."

The taste of limes puckered Khalid's mouth: tart and bracing. He was right.

"The truth conceals more than it reveals," Dimitri acknowledged reluctantly. "Point to the Amir."

"What game do you want to play with Mike?" Nimchuk rumbled.

"Not a game like this," Dayan said quickly. Too quickly. "No winners or losers."

"We seek a fair bargain," Dimitri emphasized.

Khalid's throat clenched. Faerie bargains were never "fair" by human reckoning. He'd learned that centuries ago. These vila wouldn't hesitate to use Amy to get what they wanted from her brother.

"Out of the question," Khalid said.

"Hear them out," Nimchuk said. "What do you offer? What do you want?"

Khalid bit his tongue. The wolf was right, but his interjection was nevertheless unwelcome. No one ever really benefitted from a fae exchange. There was always collateral damage, and Amy was far too close to the vila's target.

"We simply wish to invite the changeling to visit the Taiga and meet Lord Num. If Michael Arnold is indeed Zephyr's son, Num will welcome the chance to expiate the debt he owes Eurus."

Dayan's statement tasted overly sweet, and Khalid's mouth watered at the words left out. Nimchuk must have experienced a similar sensation because one blond eyebrow arched high.

"So you keep his presence a secret from Eurus, whom you claim to follow," the wolf noted.

"We serve Lord Num," Dimitri said, and the cleansing flavor of iced melon cleared Khalid's palate.

"You hope to lure the East Wind out of the desert and back to the Taiga," Malik announced.

"See." Dayan spread his arms wide. "A win-win for all of us!"

"No!" Khalid snapped. "You may not kidnap Michael Arnold as a bartering chit."

"Al-Amir, hear them out," Malik whispered. "The truth-teller can gain much from the favor of the fae. And we are freed—"

Khalid shook his head, his personal power sparking with his agitation. "No one gains *anything* from the favor of the fae! I will *not* subject Doctor Amy to such a bargain!"

Nimchuk tilted his head as he examined Khalid, but Khalid ignored his attention as he moved to the carpet's edge to have an unobstructed view of the vila.

"Michael Arnold will be our honored guest, just as he is yours," Dimitri said smoothly. "And Eurus—"

"Enough, Dimitri," Dayan said, floating out of the water. "We are bargaining with the wrong party. Let us go and speak with the changeling's sister instead."

Without thought, without reflection, Khalid cast. Battle magick was pure power, raw and unhinged, barely contained within the confines of a spell structure. The Hammer of God coalesced, arcing outward in a sweeping blow.

5

ABU DHABI, ARABIA

THE SPARKS THROWN off Khalid's coiled hammer contained enough energy to set the wooden walkway on fire. But his spell never reached his target. Whether in man- or wolf-form, Amy's vizier could move nearly as fast as the wind itself.

Nimchuk leapt in front of him, and six gigajoules of compressed magick dissipated harmlessly against the were-spell as if Nimchuk had cast the perfect anvil counterspell.

Even as it failed, Khalid began sketching the lines of the spell again.

"Amir, no!" Malik cried, grabbing his arm.

"You're right, Dayan," Dimitri said, rising out of the water as if nothing were happening. "Clearly, we are speaking with the wrong party. We must go and bargain with Amy Bant..."

The vila may have kept talking, but Khalid couldn't hear him anymore. The world had gone red with his rage. All he saw was the shade of red that wiped all magick from the world. He was unmanned but not helpless.

Khalid shook off his vizier's hand and leapt at the pair.

Arms like iron rods grabbed him, and he flailed futilely within Nimchuk's grip until his ears registered sound again and his eyes cleared.

"Al-Amir, Khalid! Stop! What have you done to him?"

Malik's voice seemed far away. The blood pounding in Khalid's ears was louder than the djinni he'd foolishly dispersed.

"I should have armed the djinni," Khalid mumbled. He was unable to fight the vila's spell any longer. "Should have killed them both."

"And you alongside us?" Dimitri asked.

"Anything. Anything to save her." Khalid felt broken. He would give anything for her, do anything for her. That was the truth.

"A tied score," Dayan clapped his hands together in glee. "Who will be the next to falter?"

"Release your spell," Malik ordered.

"Why?" Dayan asked in honest confusion. "The game's not yet won."

"A forfeit?" Dimitri asked brightly. "We accept."

"No." Nimchuk's voice was a rumble against Khalid's head. The were was holding him too tightly. "We will finish the game. The Amir will not lose control again."

"Khalid, Khalid!" Malik whispered urgently. "Enough already. She's beautiful and skilled and powerful. But she is *not* worth your life."

"She is my everything." Khalid's voice broke, and he wished he could stop speaking.

Nimchuk loosened his hold enough for Khalid to step back but didn't release him. "What if Amy refuses you, rejects you?"

The only thing worse than being spurned by the doctor would be if he had never met her at all. The taste of pickled fruit puckered his mouth with a sour sweetness that demanded his response, but Malik jerked him out of the were's grasp before he could say anything else.

"That's enough!" Malik said. "You offered to bargain on our behalf, not steal our secrets! Amir Khalid has said enough, shared enough! He's given more to our people than they have a right to, and I won't let you badger him into saying more."

The tantalizing flavor of sweetened limes surrounded them, but the faerie spell now had Malik in its sights.

Malik suddenly turned Khalid so they were facing each other. The Prime Minister ground his teeth to suppress the truths the fae spell would rip from him, but the magick was too powerful.

"That American is not worth your devotion!" Malik spat.

Khalid recoiled as if his friend had slapped him.

"She's no better than that spoiled brat of Loujain's!" Malik continued urgently. "Why do you waste your time and effort on people who aren't worthy of your attention? Farouk is not half the man you were when you were half his age!"

Khalid blinked in surprise. "Farouk cast the djinn swarm spell. He's only twenty-four years old and managed one of the most complex spells devised—"

"Because you have been training him, grooming him non-stop for this one spell! He hasn't a tenth of your resolve, your skill—"

Khalid waved Malik's words away. "He hasn't needed to! That is the gift we give the next generation — the gift of peace to be the spoiled children we couldn't be."

"And your Amy isn't spoiled, is she?" Dmitri's sly question slid through the clearing like vinegar poured into oil.

"My Amy shines with power, but her heart beats with purpose—"

"Forfeit now," Dimitri interrupted Khalid, "And we will never seek to meet her, never seek a bargain with her."

"There will be no forfeit!" Nimchuk growled, his face contorted with suppressed fury. The faerie spell was getting to all of them. It wrapped around them, prying from their hearts the feelings that words usually hid.

"Al-Amir, she isn't worthy of you!" Malik pleaded. "She knows nothing of sacrifice or duty. Her childhood was as easy as Farouk's—"

"Her father was murdered when she was three, and her mother transitioned into a siren. There is no easy life for an orphan!" Khalid snapped.

"She wasn't orphaned, Amir," Nimchuk said quietly, but his cheek twitched with his effort to remain calm. "Nor abandoned and forgotten. Her mother did not give her up. Some of the Bant resolve must come from that. They cannot let go of what they truly desire to hold." His face twisted, and he abruptly transformed in a shimmer of gold into his wolf-form.

He tilted his head upward and howled, a mournful note that seemed to echo off the brackish water beneath them. Khalid wondered what truth he'd changed form to avoid admitting.

Dayan smiled. "A forfeit!"

Khalid's ears popped as Dayan's vacuum spell dissolved. The sudden sound of water rippling and the leaves rasping in the light wind seemed quite loud after the absence of ambient noise.

"The game is ours!" Dimitri said, high-fiving Dayan, who somersaulted backward in the air.

The sound of hands clapping startled even the two faeries, and they twisted around to identify the source.

"Bravo, my boys!"

The sound ricocheted around the glade, and Khalid stiffened. *Eurus!* By the look of terror on the vila's faces, it seemed like the East Wind frightened Dimitri and Dayan as much as she frightened him.

Eurus manifested near the edge of the circle. Her long white face and pupilless eyes pressed out from the light breeze, followed by her thin body. Even before she finished materializing, she began to pace around the perimeter, fondling and petting the mangrove leaves. Not even the wind elemental could resist the allure of a fae forest.

Nimchuk sparkled back into human form, his yellow eyes tracking the East Wind's movements as she examined the changes in the forest wrought by the woodwife's spell.

"Did your game match the magnificence of this gift?" Eurus turned back to face Khalid. "I would usually be able to judge for myself, but this is the second time today my vila have sought privacy."

Nimchuk shrugged. "We are not sore losers to object to a game once it's done."

"But some games are more enjoyable than others, and I don't think this was the one you came here to play." Eurus smiled at Khalid. "A djinn swarm! Your nephew exceeded my expectations. Congratulations."

Khalid forced a smile. "Farouk exceeded many people's expectations tonight. At least his detractors will be silenced for a time."

He didn't look at Malik but felt his friend's presence at his back. They had both revealed too much tonight, but had spent too many centuries together to allow the enemy to divide them.

Eurus crossed her arms over her chest as she examined Dimitri and Dayan. "Your triumph tonight makes me wonder if you'll also manage to exceed my expectations. So few are able to give me a good game, and it's my turn to play."

The vila exchanged a quick glance before nodding. Challenge accepted. Though, Khalid doubted they had a choice.

"Lady Eurus, we have too many obligations in Riyadh to remain here and referee your match," Nimchuk said carefully. The wolf's shoulders were tight.

Eurus's smile didn't falter. "If you could enjoy a fair fight without a referee, so can we. Isn't that right, boys?"

Dimitri nodded. Dayan sighed. Neither seemed happy, but they now appeared more resigned than frightened.

Which was reasonable, Khalid supposed. They'd hoped to lure Eurus home and were about to lose their information advantage. He knew he should be disappointed that he'd lost this opportunity to extricate the fae from Arabia, but honestly, he was relieved.

The East Wind was far more dangerous than the vila, of course. But she was still fascinated by his djinni, still obsessed with the idea of a living djinn. While Khalid could protect Amy from Eurus, he wasn't sure he'd be able to guard her from any other faerie.

It took a few more minutes of careful farewells before they settled back on the carpet and left the newly-fae forest behind them. There was a burst of scent: pine resin and wine, then the air was blessedly free of any odor at all.

"That could have gone worse," Nimchuk said.

Malik shook his head. "And it could have gone better. But we have the information we needed."

Nimchuk grimaced. "I should be with Mike when Eurus comes to visit. The faster we get back to Riyadh, the better."

Khalid gestured, and the pilot obligingly maxed their speed.

"Let's hope your forest revived Dimitri and Dayan enough to last the night against her," Malik said, unfocusing his eyes as he looked at Nimchuk. "That spell ripped me raw. You must still be feeling its effects."

Nimchuk shrugged, but Khalid could see how the fae spell twined around the werewolf. The packleader had changed forms to avoid sharing his own twisted truths, but wasn't yet free of their magick.

"Speaking those words aloud was..." Malik's voice trailed off as he stared out at the still-dark city. "—illuminating in some respects. I have perhaps been hasty in my judgments, Khalid."

Khalid clasped his friend's shoulder, squeezing it slightly, before letting his hand fall. He watched buildings blur into sand dunes as they reached the city's edge. Malik had been looking out for him almost since it all began. Back when they were both too young to shave. Far too young to have been leading armies.

War and work had been all he'd known for too long. Though until now, he'd never thought of spellcraft as actual work. Something was very wrong with him.

"That game was a missed opportunity," Khalid said, and frowned. The vila's spell must still be coating his tongue. Even though he didn't taste anything, he was still speaking out of turn.

"What opportunity did we miss, Al-Amir?" Malik asked.

"I am—" Khalid hesitated. "Not myself. The jaguars are right to question me. My odd temper is another reason to be grateful Farouk managed to cast my djinn spell tonight."

"There's nothing wrong with you," Malik said.

"You're too loyal," Khalid replied sharply. "If we had to play a truth-teller's game, I wish the vila had pulled the spells from my skin to find out what's wrong with me!"

"Al-Amir, there is no spell on you. You've looked. I've looked. Faiza looked. None of us saw anything."

Khalid just shook his head. Tonight, he'd realized just how insane this attachment was.

"You think someone cast a love spell on you?" Nimchuk barked a rough laugh. "Why? Because you're prepared to give up your kingdom for her? Because the thought of her makes your cock hard and turns your brain to mush?" The wolf's face twisted. "Welcome to the club."

Khalid stared at Nimchuk. "Surely this isn't normal!"

Malik smiled gently. "Perhaps your youth on the battle-field, the pressure of ruling, left no room in your heart for such things until now. Despite her American origins, she might well be the only mage alive whose power surpasses your own."

"I don't love her because she's powerful," Khalid snapped, and regretted it. Malik was only trying to help. "It must be a spell. There's no other logical explanation."

"What does logic have to do with it?" Nimchuk scoffed. "Even if she spurns you, you'll love her still. That's not a spell. That's just being a man."

"A man?" Khalid was taken aback.

"My siren lover does not love me as much as I love her, but it doesn't matter." Nimchuk's face suddenly contorted with grief. "I love her. And one day, Cordelia will leave me for good, but even that doesn't matter. All that matters is that I love her."

The layers of fae magick that had followed them out of the forest finally blew off with Nimchuk's bleak confession. The wolf nodded at Khalid, then fixed his gaze on the starlit dunes.

It was odd. In that moment, Khalid felt a greater kinship with this American werewolf he'd known for only a few hours than he did with Malik, whom he'd known for centuries. Whether or not Amy loved him, he loved her, and that would have to be enough.

ACKNOWLEDGMENTS

Many thanks to all the people who helped bring this story duo to fruition, including Brandy, Lottie, Mark, Carol, Rena, Lisa, Jason, Jannie, and the awesome writers of Women Who Write: Laurie, Mary, Doris, and Pat. I'm serious when I say that without you, this book wouldn't be anywhere near as good as it is. Finally, a special thanks to the editors of the Wandering Wave Press for believing in my series.

AUTHOR'S NOTE

Check out my website at https://lauraengelhardt.com for fun extras like character lists, maps, and music playlists.

If you haven't already read the books in the *Fifth Mage War* series, it's best to dive in with *Sirens Unbound* or *Desert Enchantments*.

The Fifth Mage War Series

1. *Sirens Unbound*
2. *Mages Unbound*
3. *Mississippi Missing*

Short Stories and Novellas

- *Swimming Lessons*
- *Breakthrough: The War for Rio*
- *Desert Enchantments: Stories of the Djinn Dictator*

www.ingramcontent.com/pod-product-compliance
Lightning Source LLC
Chambersburg PA
CBHW030541130626
46552CB00006B/2370